HAUNTING CHARLIE

WITCHES OF PALMETTO POINT BOOK 1

WENDY WANG

CHAPTER 1

Charlie Payne picked up the empty file folder and fanned herself. A quiet buzz from the fluorescent lights droned above, and she fought the urge to close her eyes.

"Yes, ma'am," she said into her headset. "I absolutely understand, and I am so sorry that's happened to you."

She let the customer rattle on for another thirty seconds before straightening up and forcing herself to wake up. Why did they have to keep this office so damn hot during the spring? It's not like she lived in New York or Minnesota or some state that constantly lived under the threat of snow until May. They needed to turn the damn heat off.

"Yes, ma'am I totally understand. Let me tell you what

I can do for you because I want to resolve this. We want happy customers."

As if on cue, her supervisor Dylan stepped up to the half-wall of her cubicle and stared down at her. He barely looked fifteen years old, with his One Direction hair and his freshly scrubbed, acne-ridden skin. He was really in his early twenties and had a degree in management from a school she'd never heard of—and constantly reminded his underlings about it. He dragged his forefingers across his lips into a curve while mouthing the word *smile*. Then he pointed to a poster on the wall of a big fat yellow smiley face. The caption read: *Are you smiling? Customers can hear it in your voice when you don't.* Fighting the urge to roll her eyes, she clenched her jaw and forced a very fake smile for his benefit.

"Yes, ma'am I am happy to give you a credit to cover those fees," she said meeting, Dylan's gaze, daring him to question her solution. Refunding fees was supposed to be a last resort. He pursed his lips, but didn't say anything. As he walked away, she stopped typing and turned her right hand up flipping the bird at him in the narrow space between her keyboard tray and the desk. "I just need to verify some information."

Her cell phone buzzed next to her keyboard, and she glanced down. The text was from her cousin Daphne.

"I just need your date of birth." She kept talking but her fingers twitched, wanting to pick up her cell and concentrate on the text. "Alright-y then. I'll just credit those fees back to your account. It may take a few days for it to show up on your statement, and I just need to remind you that to avoid the fees in the future, you'll need to maintain a daily balance of at least a thousand dollars." The reminder was automatic since she said it more times than she could count in a day. "Is there anything else I can do for you today ma'am?" With her customer sounding much happier than when she first called, Charlie picked up her phone so she could get a better look. "Well, alright-y then, you have a wonderful day and thank you for calling Bel-Com Credit Union."

The text simply read: Text me on your break. I have a proposition for you.

A proposition. She sighed. Her cousin was always coming up with crazy schemes and was always wanting to drag Charlie, and her other two cousins, along. Still... sometimes there was fun involved. The four of them had taken a cruise to the Bahamas last fall because of one of Daphne's propositions. Charlie suddenly felt eyes on the back of her neck. She glanced over her shoulder and her heart jumped into her throat. Her hand flew up to her chest. "Oh, my God, you startled me." Dylan stood right behind her, glaring at the phone in her hand.

"Charlotte—you know the rules about cell phones. Please don't make me write you up. I hate writing people up."

Lie! She forced herself not to roll her eyes at him. Dylan had written up more people than all the other supervisors combined. His last write-up had even killed one of her coworkers. Poor Helen Jackson had died from a heart attack after Dylan wrote her up for the second time. The call center had a three strikes policy. One more write-up and Helen would've been out. If she had lived. Instead, she went into the women's bathroom to have a good cry and ended up dead. Not exactly a great way to go out.

"Yes, I do, Dylan." Charlie tucked her cell into her back pocket and laid her headset on the desk. Her fingers deftly entered the appropriate break code on her phone and she stood up. At five-foot-ten she towered over him. Staring down her nose at him was the only thing pleasurable about working for the little twerp. "Cell phones are only allowed to be out on breaks and lunches." She grabbed her purse from the file cabinet drawer and slung it over her shoulder. "I guess it's a good thing I'm going to lunch."

Dylan scowled and folded his arms across his skinny chest. "Yes, I suppose it is."

"See you in thirty." She walked away, leaving him to stare after her.

CHAPTER 2

C harlie grabbed her lunch bag from the fridge in the break room and took a seat at one of the back tables away from the floor-to-ceiling windows. The whole building had them and they overlooked the Ashley River. The view was supposed to be a perk ,but, in her opinion, the tall glass only amplified the heat.

The large room filled with long tables was almost empty for this time of day. She usually had a late lunch so she'd miss the lines competing for one of the four microwaves. The only company she had were two women from another department. They must have been on a break because they each had a soda and only one appeared to be eating from a small bag of nuts.

Charlie pulled out her salad in a jar and turkey sandwich and then texted Daphne.

What's up?

She shook the jar, dispersing the dressing evenly before opening it, and speared the top leaves with her plastic fork. Sure, she could have used one of the paper plates provided in the break room, but she was too lazy and hated to add more crap to the landfill than necessary. She stared at the text screen while she unwrapped her sandwich and took the first bite. Three little animated dots told her Daphne was typing. Finally, the text appeared.

Breakfast Friday with me, Lisa, and Jen?

She picked up her phone deftly moving across the text keys with her thumbs.

Sure. What time?

The three dots mesmerized her.

7:00 a.m.

Charlie switched over to her calendar app to check her schedule. Her call center gave out schedules a month in advance, which was not a lot of time to plan, but better than nothing. She had friends in the business who only got two weeks. Talk about hard to plan your life. She didn't have to be in until 12:30 that day. That would work.

7 sounds good.

Cool. I have something I need you to help me with.

What?

Don't want to say in a text.

Okaaaay...just tell me this. It's not illegal, is it? ;)

No.

And no one's dying, right?

Hahahaha. No. No way. That would warrant an actual phone call.

God forbid you actually use the phone for its intended purpose. LOL.

Nobody LOL's anymore.

Are you throwing shade at me about my age?

Hahaha (appropriate response).

Brat, she thought. She wasn't that much older than Daphne. Only six years. She sighed and scowled at the screen.

Fine. I'll see y'all Friday morning. She started to insert the tongue-out emoji, but stopped herself. Would that make her seem even older? *Screw it,* she thought and typed it in anyway.

A woman stopped in front of her table. "Excuse me, you're Charlotte, right?" The woman glanced over her shoulder, her dark gaze flitting around the room. She leaned forward, pressing one hand, palm down, on the table and whispered, "Someone told me something about you—"

Charlie clenched her teeth to hold onto her smile. She didn't have to be psychic to know what came next. "Oh?"

"They said that you were—" She chewed on her bottom lip. "They said that you could see things. Future things."

"Oh." Charlie put her phone on the table. "What is your name?"

"Emily. Emily Hager."

"Why don't you have a seat?" Charlie softened her face trying to be as approachable as possible.

"I don't mean to bother you." Emily pushed her shoulder-length brown hair behind one ear.

Charlie noticed the two women near the window. They leaned in, whispering to each other, watching the exchange between Charlie and Emily with great interest. "You're not bothering me. But I can't help you unless you sit down and talk to me a little bit."

Emily pulled out the chair, dragging it across the linoleum with a painful scraping noise that always set Charlie's teeth on edge. She sat down and placed the bag of chips she'd gotten from one of the vending machines on the table. She folded her chubby hands in front of her. Her dark brown eyes settled on Charlie, unwavering.

"May I ask who *they* are?" Charlie said leaning forward with her arms on the table.

"A few of the women I work with," Emily said.

"I see. What department do you work in?"

"I'm an accounts auditor," she said.

"Well, it's very nice to meet you. Did someone direct you to my website?"

Emily hesitated, her throat bobbing. She nodded.

"Are you interested in having a reading, or is something else going on?"

"I just—I don't know what I'm doing here." A nervous titter bubbled up, and she covered her mouth. "I don't even think I believe in this stuff. But—"

Charlie reached across the table and placed her hand on top of Emily's wrist. As soon as she touched the woman, it was like opening a high definition 3-D video channel into the woman's life. Emily caught eating ice cream in a dimly lit kitchen. Emily's fingers tightening around the spoon in her hand, instead of grabbing a knife from the block on the counter, while her husband shouts, "And you wonder why I don't want to fuck you!" Charlie's eyes flew open. Why she always saw into the dark heart of people she didn't know. She blinked away the images, struggling to smile.

"Are you okay?" Emily asked.

Charlie nodded and cleared her throat. "You know, I normally don't give readings for people I work with."

"I see—" Emily pulled her arm away, pressing it close to her chest. "Is it money? You want your fee?"

"No." Charlie shook her head. "God, no. Nothing like that. It's just—here's the thing—I can be wrong, in fact, I am wrong a lot, and I don't want you to make any rash decisions based on some conversation we had in the lunchroom."

"Oh." Emily's round face deflated with disappointment.

Charlie sighed. Giving the reading was the easy part—the hard part was knowing what to divulge. Should she tell Emily that staying with her husband could lead to ruination? One thing she had learned over the years was that when someone like Emily came to her for help, the woman would listen, which Charlie found utterly crazy sometimes. She was a complete stranger, and yet this woman wanted to hang her whole life, her future, on whatever words came out of Charlie's mouth. The power of it could change lives, and it scared the bejesus out of her. There were no guarantees what she saw would actually come true. None. Charlie took a deep breath and stretched out her hand.

"I need you to take my hand. Just for a minute. Then I'm going to ask you a few questions, and I just want you to just answer yes or no. Is that okay?"

Emily sucked her bottom lip into her mouth and nodded, placing her hand in Charlie's. Charlie closed her eyes and concentrated. After a few seconds, she released Emily's hand and let the vision unfold—Emily in a Sunday dress, going to a new church. Emily singing in the choir, laughing with a man with a silver beard. He was older than her by at least ten years, but Emily didn't care because he made her feel beautiful. He bought her an ice cream cone and kissed her. Then in a flash he was holding a baby in a hospital room while Emily slept after a hard day of labor.

Charlie blew out a breath and opened her eyes.

"Do you love your husband?"

An array of emotions darted across Emily's face before sadness pulled at the corners of her mouth. She shook her head. "No. I don't think I do. Not anymore."

"He makes you feel…small? Inconsequential? Ugly?"

Emily's bottom lip escaped her mouth and trembled. Her voice dropped to a whisper and shame burned a path across her cheeks. "Yes."

"Emily, how old are you?"

Confusion filled Emily's tiny, blue eyes. "I don't know how to answer yes or no to that."

"Sorry." Charlie gave her an apologetic smile. "You can answer that one."

"I'll be thirty-five next month."

"All right, then. In the interest of biological clocks, I'm going to tell you what I see, but just know that sometimes I'm wrong."

"Okay." Emily's expectant gaze didn't waver.

Charlie took a deep breath, trying to decide what to filter and what to lay bare. "If you leave your husband, it will make you happy but—"

The lines around Emily's mouth deepened forming a pair of parenthesis. "But?"

"But only if you go to a new church. Does that make sense to you? Your real happiness will be found in a new church. Singing in the choir. That's where you'll find the greatest love of your life."

Emily's brow smoothed and her face became lighter. "Singing in the choir?"

"Yes."

"So, I should just leave him and join a new church?"

"Yes."

"Are you telling me to give it all to the Lord? Or—I think I'm confused."

Charlie smiled, anxiety coiling around her heart. She didn't want to be wrong. Emily's freedom depended on it. "Yes. Give it all to the Lord, Emily. Join a new church and sing your heart out." The man from Charlie's vision appeared in her head again—so taken by Emily and her faith that he loved her almost immediately. "Your faith will lead you to happiness."

Emily sat back, her face becoming thoughtful. A smile stretched across her lips. "Thank you. Thank you so much."

"Don't thank me yet. Like I said—" Charlie shrugged. "—I can be wrong. Thank me in five years."

"I will." Emily rose from her chair, still grinning.

Charlie watched Emily walk away, lightness filling

each step. Charlie took the last bite of her sandwich, hoping to God she had not just ruined the woman's life.

* * *

CHARLIE HID IN THE LAST STALL OF THE WOMEN'S bathroom during her last break of the day. Becky Henstridge was recruiting for the department's bake sale, and she just didn't want to deal with the woman's unflinching persistence. Becky would ask and ask until she finally wore her victim down. In her heart, Charlie wanted to contribute, but this month was going to be a little tight, and from past experience, Becky wouldn't care. The woman wouldn't relent until Charlie said yes, which she just couldn't do right now. She'd been working tons of overtime, saving every penny since she and Scott had separated—all for a down payment on a condo. A place of her own. Paid for with her own money, not her husband's.

Ex-husband, she reminded herself. They'd signed all the papers making it official almost a year ago, and the dull ache in her chest was finally starting to fade.

Her phone buzzed in her pocket. Her ten-minute break was almost up. An hour and a half and she could go home. She flushed the toilet, just in case someone walked in as she left the stall. It was stupid that she cared about what these people thought, but she did have to work with them every day.

She leaned toward the mirror and sighed. When she'd left her house this morning, her fine, blonde hair had been pulled into a neat ponytail. Over the course of a day of putting on and taking off her headset, though, stray bits of hair had pulled out, forming a crazy pale halo around her face. The lavender shadows beneath her eyes were beginning to show through her now fading make-up. She rarely slept more than four or five hours a night anymore because of the damned dreams.

After turning on the cold spigot, she pumped out some liquid soap and scrubbed her hands together till the soap lathered. Even if she never used the toilet, she always washed her hands. Just the idea of the germs in this place gave her the heebie-jeebies. Her gaze drifted back up to the mirror to find Helen Jackson leaning against one of the stall dividers behind her. A yelp ushered out of Charlie's mouth.

"Jesus, Helen. We've already had this conversation. You're dead. You need to just find a light and walk toward it," Charlie snapped. She cast a quick glance at the door, hoping no one was close enough to hear.

Helen looked almost exactly the same as she had the day she died. Her short salt-and-pepper hair was styled and, even dead, she still rocked business casual—with black slacks, black flats and a red blouse that set off nicely against her dark skin. Only Helen was not quite as solid as she once was.

"You think I want to be in this bathroom?" Helen threw up her arms in an animated fashion. "I should be in the churchyard. Or at the very least haunting that little pimply faced supervisor. Instead, I'm trapped in here. Lawd, I don't know what I did to deserve this!"

Charlie finished rinsing her hands and pulled a paper towel from the dispenser.

"I'm sorry," she said. "It must really suck being stuck in here."

"Well, that's an understatement if I've ever heard one," Helen grumbled. Her lips twisted into a grimace. "How come you can see me? Nobody else can. They walk right through me. Sit right down on top of me. Ain't nothing more shocking than to be sitting on the toilet thinking about the afterlife and have some big old girl come in and sit down on top of you with her naked butt."

Charlie laughed out loud.

Anger flashed across Helen's face. "It ain't funny."

"No," Charlie said covering her mouth and biting the insides of her cheeks to stop from smiling. "You're right, it's not—" She gave Helen a sideways glance. "It may be a little funny."

"No!" Helen protested, holding up her hand, one finger pointed toward the sky.

"Okay. Okay. You're right, I'm sorry. It's not funny at

all." Charlie sighed and leaned against the counter. She folded her arms across her chest. "You know, I don't really know why I can see you. Maybe it's because I come from a family that has more people like me than like you."

"What? Dead people?"

"No. Normal people. I've just been seeing dead people since I was little girl."

"And you ain't scared? Lawd, if I saw a dead person when I was alive, I'd have lost my mind." Helen fanned herself with her hand. Charlie was tempted to ask her if she was hot too, but she knew the spirit's reactions were more about habit than anything else. "My grandma would've called you a witch."

"Well, according to my ex-husband, your grandma would've been right." Charlie winked. "It was good to see you, Helen. You take care and avoid being sat on. My break is almost over, and I don't want to be written up."

"Lawd, no. We don't want that," Helen said. "I don't think there's enough room in here for the both of us."

CHAPTER 3

C harlie rose early on Friday to miss the morning traffic in Charleston. Once she left West Ashley, she sped down Highway-17 headed toward Talmadge Island to meet her cousins for breakfast.

Charlie turned onto Market Street, the main thoroughfare of the little town of Palmetto Point. After her parents died, she went to live with her grandmother and knew the town well.

The island locals were mainly made up of a mix of wealthy retirees and families that had been on the island for generations. The official downtown area spanned barely five blocks, but was chock full of thriving businesses. The town was just small enough to have staved off the invasion of larger chain stores, which along with its quaint and well-manicured streets, gave a sense of stepping back in time. Parking spaces lined the street in front of the array of businesses and Charlie pulled into a prime spot in front of her cousin's restaurant, The Kitchen Witch Café.

When she entered, the bell over the door rang and the scent of banana pancakes and bacon rushed over her senses. Once inside the bustling restaurant, she glanced around. The place was packed, and the tables filled with people taking advantage of six a.m. to eight a.m., buy one-get one half-off breakfast specials. Only a few spaces at the counter remained empty.

Charlie waved at the woman behind the cash register —her cousin Jen Holloway. Jen's dark pixie haircut with magenta fringed bangs framed her heart-shaped face perfectly.

Jen returned a wave and a wide grin spread across her full lips. "Hey, cuz."

"Looks like business is booming." Charlie suppressed the twinge of jealousy at her cousin's success. The Kitchen Witch was one of the busiest and most popular restaurants on the island.

"It's always kinda crazy on Fridays because of the specials. Daphne's already here. She's holed up in the last booth, so we can have some privacy." Jen pointed to their younger cousin.

Charlie wasn't sure how much real privacy they were

going to get in a place this busy. Hopefully the noise would help.

"Lisa just texted me she should be here in a few minutes. Why don't you go sit down?" Jen handed Charlie a menu, and she hesitated.

"What's wrong?" Jen asked.

"Nothing. I just—I just didn't think this through. I'm trying not to spend any extra money this month."

"Honey, don't worry about it, okay? Family eats free, now what do you want to drink?"

"Jen," Charlie protested.

"Don't argue."

Normally, she'd be a little embarrassed about her predicament. She had actually planned to come and sit. Maybe drink some tea or coffee. If she'd been with normal people, she would've said she was on a diet, but her cousins were like her—they could all see through a lie. It was, as her cousin Lisa liked to say, their super power.

"Fine," Charlie relented. "But I'll pay you back. I don't know when but I will pay you back. I promise."

"Sure," Jen said. Her blue eyes glittered with mischief. "I'll let you come and babysit Ruby for me sometime."

"I thought your dad took care of Ruby for you."

"You're right. Then you can babysit my dad."

"Well, he needs it, I guess," Charlie teased.

"He sure does." Jen grinned. "Now what do you want to drink? Coffee, iced tea? Orange juice?"

"Coffee sounds good."

"Coming right up, now go sit down."

"Yes, ma'am." Charlie made her way to the booth and took a seat next to Daphne. Her cousin didn't even look up from her phone. Charlie snapped her fingers in the space between Daphne's face and her screen.

"Hey—" Daphne scowled, protesting before finally looking up. "Oh. Hey. When did you get here?"

"Good morning to you too," Charlie said. "I've been here ten minutes. You didn't even notice?"

"Liar." Daphne's cheeks pinked, and she pushed her hair behind one ear. She laid her phone on the table with the screen facing down. "I guess we're just waiting for Lisa."

"Uh-huh," Charlie said, smiling at her younger cousin. The resemblance was so strong between Daphne and Jen they could've been sisters, with their deep brunette hair, large, blue eyes, and impish features. "So, did you do Jen's hair?"

"Of course." Daphne laid her arm across the table and rested her hand across the back of her phone. Charlie suppressed the urge to grin and shake her head. The girl just couldn't live one second without her phone in her hand. "I could do something similar for you. Maybe a pink stripe."

Charlie laughed it off. "I don't think so."

"Come on—you know you want a pink stripe. Something that screams 'I'm available and in my sexual prime, boys.'"

Charlie's cheeks burned, and she shook her head. "No. That is absolutely not what I want."

Daphne shrugged one slender shoulder. "Suit yourself. But the offer stands."

"Thanks. I'll keep it in mind." Charlie's gaze drifted to the counter where she watched Jen remove her black apron and put it in one of the cubbyholes underneath the counter.

"Evangeline," Jen said loud enough that Charlie and Daphne could hear her. "Can you take over for me out here please?"

A minute later, an older woman emerged from the kitchen wearing a black apron. Her long silver hair was pinned up in a messy bun and she glanced over at the table and waved.

"Hey, Evangeline," Charlie said.

"Hey, Mama," Daphne said.

Evangeline smiled and the skin around her eyes crinkled. "Hey, girls."

"Your mama looks good," Charlie said.

"Yes, she does. You know, I have girls younger than me begging me to make their hair that color," Daphne said.

At twenty-six she owned the most popular hair salon in town.

All her cousins were successful—either owning their own business or having a profession. And what was she? A call center worker. She wasn't complaining, really. It was good job. It paid the bills, and she had the all-important health insurance. With overtime, she'd managed to save over ten thousand dollars for a down payment in just over a year. But there had to be more than just waking up and going to work, coming home, and vegging in front of the television. If she disappeared tomorrow, they'd just replace her with someone else as fast as they could.

Jen sat across from them and they got the niceties out of the way—asking about children, and work, and Charlie told them about the condo she'd put an offer on.

"That's great!" Daphne said. "We should definitely celebrate."

"Well, they haven't accepted the offer yet," she said, dosing her coffee with milk and sugar. "Hopefully I'll hear today, and if they do accept it, I don't know how much the closing costs are going to be yet, so I'm being stingy till I hear one way or the other."

"I am so happy for you. I know how hard it's been having to start over," Daphne said

"It's fine." Charlie said, fidgeting with the edges of the menu.

"Well, I'm proud of you," Jen said.

"Should I be proud too?" Lisa said, approaching the table. Lisa was dressed in a smart gray skirt, a silky, pale yellow blouse that set off well against her long, strawberry-blonde hair.

"Absolutely," Jen said. "Charlie's buying a condo."

"That's awesome Charlie—" Lisa started to sit, but Jen pushed her way out.

"No," Jen said. "You take the inside."

"I hate the inside," Lisa said.

"I know, but if Evangeline needs me, you'll to have to keep moving in and out. You know how crazy that would make you."

"I guess," Lisa said, scowling at her sister. She slid inside the booth and gave Charlie and Daphne a smile. "It's good to see you girls. I don't think I've seen you since Christmas, Charlie."

"I know." Charlie fidgeted. "It's been hectic. I've been working a lot of overtime."

"All right, well, let me know when you close on your condo, and I'll go with you."

"Really? I'd love that. I hate having to deal with all the legal stuff."

"Well, that's the thing about having a cousin who's a lawyer, you get your legal advice for free." Lisa winked.

"I really appreciate that," Charlie said. "But, they haven't even accepted my offer yet."

"Still, when they do—" Lisa picked up a menu and began perusing it. "What's good?"

Jen signaled to one of the waitresses and got their orders out of the way. Lisa folded her hands on the table and shifted her gaze to their youngest cousin.

"All right, Daphne." Lisa used her most lawyerly voice. "It's your show. What's so important that you couldn't just say it in a text?"

Daphne glanced into each of their faces before finally settling her gaze on Charlie. "Well, I have a problem—"

"Oh, no. Sweetie, are you okay?" Jen put her hand over Daphne's and concern etched her forehead.

"Me? Oh, I'm fine. It's not my problem exactly. It's a client of mine."

"A client?" Lisa said, sounding dubious. She narrowed her hazel eyes. "I'm not sure exactly how we can help one of your clients. You're the expert on hair."

Daphne shook her head. "It's not that kind of problem. It's more of a—" She glanced around, making sure no one around them was paying attention and whispered, "ghost problem."

Lisa and Jen groaned and sat against the back of the booth seat.

"Come on, you two, don't be like that. You haven't even heard what it is yet," Daphne whined, falling into the youngest sibling role.

Charlie's shoulders sagged, and she glanced down at

her hands. Maybe she could just slip under the table and run. The weight of their stares pinned her in place, putting any thought of escape out of reach. She took a deep breath and looked Daphne in the eye. "What kind of ghost problem are we talking about, exactly?"

"Well, I have this client—Susan Tate. She recently inherited Talmadge House."

"No. Absolutely not." Lisa's voice carried a warning. "Nope. Nope and nope."

"What? You don't even know what I'm gonna say!" Daphne protested.

"Yes, I do," Lisa said. "You want us to go clean that damned house."

"Just hear me out—" Daphne implored. "This could be really good for Charlie."

"For me? Wait, why for me?" Charlie's gaze shifted to Daphne.

"Because it would be great exposure for your business," Daphne said.

"I don't have a business," Charlie protested.

"Yes, you do. You have a website. You have a Facebook page. You take money for your services. You definitely have a business."

"Trust me, I don't need to advertise. I get plenty of people wanting readings just from word-of-mouth. Seems like everybody wants to talk to their dead Aunt Tilly or know their future." The words tasted bitter in Charlie's mouth. Sometimes she hated what she was. What she could see and hear that no one else could.

"Daphne. Why don't you concentrate on your business?" Lisa scowled. "And just leave Charlie alone."

"You are so contrary sometimes. You know that?" Daphne folded her arms across her chest. "And you!" She rounded on Charlie. "You have this awesome gift and you don't even use it to its fullest potential."

"It's really not awesome, Daphne." Charlie's cheeks grew hot, and she clenched her teeth. "Scott and I broke up because of my awesome gift, and he ended up with custody of Evan. So, whatever you think, it's really more curse than blessing."

They all grew quiet. Charlie's words hung over them like a cold, heavy mist.

"Well..." Daphne's fiddled with her spoon. Guilt wrinkled her elfin features. "I kinda already told her that you would do it."

"Dammit, Daphne," Charlie said. "You had no right to do that."

"I know. But you're not going to have to do it alone. We'll help you. Won't we?" Daphne's voice grew bossy and less contrite. She gave Jen and Lisa a pointed look. Lisa frowned and rolled her eyes.

"You are a manipulative brat," Lisa said. She sighed. "But of course, we'll help Charlie. Although, ghosts have never been my forte. Last time I dealt with a spirit it wasn't exactly friendly." Lisa's hand drifted to her head and rubbed her temple absently. Charlie bit the inside of her cheek to keep from smiling. Lisa's last encounter with a ghost had ended with a handful of silverware lobbed at her by an angry woman who was not quite ready to move onto the next plane. An antique silver fork had stabbed Lisa in the temple and blood had been spilled all over Lisa's favorite silk blouse.

Daphne smirked. "See? Even spirits recognize contrary when they see it."

"Stop it you two. I swear you're as bad as Ruby sometimes," Jen scolded."

"Between the four of us, we have plenty of power to reign in whatever is haunting that house, but only *if* " – Jen's dark blue eyes settled on Charlie— "This is something Charlie wants to do. If she doesn't, I fully support that too."

Charlie gave Jen a grateful smile. As practicing witches, her cousins had their own gifts. They weren't sensitive the way she was. None of them could see or hear spirits like she did, although there were instances where a spirit would make itself known, such as throwing things or becoming a floating ball of light. But unlike Jen, Lisa, and Daphne, Charlie had no affinity for magic. No talent for using the living world to affect the people she met. The world of the dead was a different matter, though. "I guess, it won't hurt to go talk to her,"

Charlie said. "You know, I've never been to Talmadge House."

"I have," Lisa said. "All I can say is it's depressing."

"Why clean it now?" Jen asked.

"Well, Susan wants to turn it into a bed-and-breakfast. and I have total faith we can help her so she can make that happen. And if Charlie fails, we always have Lisa."

"Me? What exactly do you expect me to do?" Lisa's brows rose half-way up her forehead and her eyes widened.

"Well, if Charlie can't make the spirits leave by asking nicely, you can get all bossy and lawyerly on them."

Jen and Charlie snickered.

"Ha-ha. Funny," Lisa said. "And what exactly are you gonna do? You gonna hold them down and give them highlights?"

"Actually, I was thinking that I would film it. We could put it up on YouTube. Then, Charlie, you could link to it on your website as another service you offer."

"Seriously?" Lisa asked. "You want to be a ghost hunter?"

"Not me. Charlie," Daphne said. "I think there's real potential here. I mean we're in one of the most haunted areas in the whole country. And I can help with all the social media stuff to market yourself."

"I don't know that I want to be marketed, Daphne," Charlie said. "I have more than just myself to think about.

I have Evan, and I don't know if my conservative banking employer would like it if I'm out ghost busting."

"Why would they care? It's not like you're doing it on their time."

"No, she's right. It's all about reputation. It may be better if you keep this sort of thing on the down low," Lisa said.

"I'm still gonna film it," Daphne said. "It's up to you whether you want to put it on your website or not. But I think it would be a great opportunity."

"Okay," Charlie said. "So, you've been there, Lisa, has it always been haunted?"

"I don't know about haunted, but it definitely has a bad vibe to it. She should just donate it to the state, if you ask me. Let them turn it into a historic site, or better yet, bulldoze it and develop the land. With the view, it's prime real estate," Lisa said.

"You would think that," Daphne muttered, rolling her eyes. She turned her attention back to Charlie. "Actually, she didn't seem to have any problems until they started doing some construction and updating the wiring."

"That sounds about right. Spirits can get restless when construction starts on a place they're haunting," Charlie said. "Anything else you want to tell me?"

"Only that she is the sweetest lady you'll ever meet, and I really just want to help her. That's all," Daphne said.

"All right," Charlie said. "I'll meet with her. On one condition."

Daphne clapped her hands together and bounced in her seat. "Anything."

"You have to go with me for the initial consultation."

"Sure. Of course. We should also take Lisa," Daphne said

"Me? Why me?" Lisa said.

"No, she's right," Charlie said. "Of all of us, you're the most logical and the one who immediately sees through any kind of bullshit."

Lisa thought it over for a moment before finally nodding. "Okay, I'll go."

"Yay, Lisa." Daphne gave her cousin an exaggerated grin. "I'll take care of all the arrangements. You won't be sorry, I promise."

Lisa glared at her younger cousin and feigned a scowl. "Don't make me tell you that I already am."

CHAPTER 4

"Ahair emergency? You have got to be kidding me!" Charlie's voice rose half an octave. It had all happened quickly. Daphne had called Susan and arranged for them to meet her on Sunday at one. It was perfect. Short of some sort of world-ending emergency, none of them had to work.

"Dammit Daphne. You promised." Charlie drove along Highway-17, heading out of West Ashley, toward Talmadge Island. "How on earth do you have a hair emergency on a Sunday?"

"I make myself available to some of my best clients on my days off on a case-by-case basis. You know, just in case," Daphne said.

"Just in case, what?"

"Things come up. I get twice my fee on a Sunday. My

client's daughter tried to dye her own hair blonde. She has brown hair. Let's just say, she could give Ronald McDonald a run for his money. Prom is next weekend, and I have to make sure it's perfect before then."
Daphne sounded as if she were about to perform brain surgery, and Charlie didn't know whether to laugh or scream.

"That is insane," Charlie muttered.

"Why? Lisa's still going. You don't have to do it by yourself. And, anyway, trust me, Susan is the nicest lady."

"Lisa is not gonna be happy that you're flaking."

"Oh, she'll get over it. My client's here. I gotta go."

"Daphne?" The line went dead and Charlie cursed under her breath. She dialed Lisa's cell and told her about Daphne.

Lisa laughed, but there was a bitter undertone. "Absolutely figures. Her client and we get stuck with it."

"You don't have to go if you don't want to."

"Don't be ridiculous. I'm not gonna abandon you. And, anyway, I'm already halfway there."

"If you're sure," Charlie said, more grateful than she could express.

"I am. I'll see you there." Lisa ended the call.

Charlie turned onto Talmadge Island Road and wound her way through the heart of the island. Her uncle Jack, Lisa and Jen's father, had a house on the other side of the island, overlooking the Stono River, and she loved to go out there and have supper sometimes, but going all the way out to Talmadge House was quite a haul.

There was something beautiful and haunting about the island's landscape. Golden marsh grass and shady back roads guarded by tall graceful live oaks draped in swaths of gray moss surrounded her. Charlie opened the sunroof of her Honda Civic. Dappled light filtered through the canopy of trees and the sulfurous odor of thick, black pluff mud from the nearby marsh wafted into the car's interior. The bursts of pink and white azaleas coloring the landscape were already starting to fade in the late-April heat. Sometimes when she came out to these old islands, she would catch spirits from the corner of her eye reliving some moment of their lives. The land out here was charged with the blood and sweat of those who had worked it. While she found these little glimpses of history fascinating, her heart ached that some part of their soul was left behind to relive things over and over again.

She followed the directions Daphne had given her, and after what seemed like forever, she found the road leading to the house. Passing beneath the great oaks lining the avenue was like stepping back in time, and she almost expected to see a horse-drawn carriage on the lane. The house rose on an expanse of lush, green lawn and faced the river. Its four white pillars stretched from the wide, front porch to the roofline and the white paint was cracked and peeling in places. A scaffold stood on the north end of the house, a reminder of the large-scale construction needed to restore it to its former glory. Behind the house were woods thick with tall pines and hardwoods. Her gaze scanned the tree line, drawn to the darkness beneath the thick canopy. Her heart beat a path to her throat when she saw them, one by one, step from the shadows. The apparitions shimmered. Gossamer and silvery, they waited—for what, she didn't know yet, but she could feel them and their allure frightened her.

Charlie pulled into the semi-circular driveway in front of the house and parked. She sat, gripping the steering wheel. The dark energy emanating from the house and woods behind it sent a wave of nausea through her. No wonder Susan Tate had been frazzled enough to reach out to Daphne.

A knock on her window almost made her jump out of her skin and she put her hand over her heart. She glared at her cousin through the glass.

"You all right?" Lisa asked.

Charlie nodded, took her keys out of the ignition, and emerged from her car. The heavy scent of early blooming jasmine coated the back of her throat.

"You sure?" Lisa sounded concerned. "You look a little pale."

Charlie focused on her cousin's freckled face. "I'm fine. Do you feel that?"

"I'm not the empath here, remember?" Lisa shrugged and scanned the front of the house. "That may work in your favor, though." She slipped her hand inside the buttery leather of her expensive handbag and pulled out a velvet box. She pushed it into Charlie's hand. "This is from Jen. She said to wear it no matter what."

Charlie flipped open the top of the jewelry box. A rough, cylindrical, black stone flanked by four polished beads dangled from a silver chain, which she recognized as hematite and tiger's eye. Charlie shifted her gaze from the necklace to her cousin's face, questioning.

"It's for protection," Lisa said. She pulled an identical one hidden inside her blouse to show Charlie.

"For protection?"

"Oh, yeah," Lisa said. "If she could have bathed us in sage, she would have."

"Well, thank God for Jen. Based on what I'm feeling from this house, we may just need it." Charlie fastened the long silver chain around her neck and slipped it inside her navy T-shirt, letting it fall between her breasts. "Let's do this."

They walked up the steps to the brick front porch and Charlie reached for the tarnished brass knocker. She paused before lifting the heavy ring. "What year did Aldus Talmadge die?"

Lisa pulled out her phone to do a quick Internet search. "Dammit."

"What?"

Lisa frowned. "There's no service out here."

"You still want to do this?" Charlie asked.

The heavy black door opened wide, startling them both. A woman with a round face and kind brown eyes emerged from the house. Her dark hair was cut in a stylish, wavy bob that made her look younger than she really was. Dressed in white seersucker, she looked more like she was going to the country club to sip wine and gossip with her girlfriends than to deal with powerful forces gathered around her house.

"You must be Charlie," she said in a drawl that didn't sound like someone from the South Carolina low country. She flashed a wide smile of perfectly white teeth. "I'm Susan Tate."

Susan took hold of Charlie's hand and shook it vigorously. Flashes of a man filled Charlie's head. Most of the time, when she met someone with a spirit attached to them, just a touch would force the spirit to materialize before her. But this man emanated darkness and Charlie got the distinct feeling he didn't want to show himself. All she could sense of him was his shape. He was tall and broad across the shoulders. A gold chain hung from his waistcoat with a fob tucked inside one of the pockets but there was no face to go with spirit.

"Yes, I am," Charlie said, gently pulling her hand out of the woman's grip. She balled her fingers into a fist and held it close to her side. Lisa gave her a sideways glance, her hazel eyes narrowing, watching her cousin's every move.

"It is so nice to meet you. You look exactly the way Daphne said you would," Susan said.

Charlie exchanged a look with her cousin. Lisa's mouth twisted, suppressing the grin threatening to break across her lips and her eyebrows lifted in a glad-it's-you-and-not-me expression.

"Good old Daphne," Lisa said.

"I thought she was joining us. Should we wait?" Susan's gaze drifted toward the road leading to the house.

"She couldn't make it today. Hair emergency," Lisa said. Charlie threw a dirty look in her cousin's direction. Lisa was enjoying this way too much.

"Oh, dear." Susan kept smiling in that way that Southern women often did when they heard news that didn't exactly please them. "I hope it's not serious."

"Oh, no," Lisa said. "Nothing that a buzz cut or a box of red hair color couldn't cure."

Susan laughed politely. "Oh, my goodness. That sounds awful."

"I'm sure it will be fine. Daphne lives for that sort of thing," Lisa said.

"Alright-y then, why don't y'all come inside and have some lemonade? We can get to know each other a little better." Susan's cheerful demeanor gave away none of the anxiety Daphne had warned them about. In typical southern fashion, she treated them as if they had just dropped by for a nice long visit and not to evaluate the forces haunting her house.

Susan led them into the foyer, a grand room with a staircase to match. The stairs curved up to a landing that split into pair of shorter stairs, leading to different wings of the house. Light filtered in from French doors on the left side of the room and it pushed the gloom into the corners, casting shadows over the stacks of boxes lining the right side of the room and down the wide hallway. Despite the dinginess of the walls and the layers of dust on the old oil paintings, the faded opulence intimidated Charlie. Gold leafing, which had once covered the crown molding, flaked in long strips in places. Even with all this damage, it was hard denying what a magnificent site it must have been.

"You have a beautiful house. Do you have a lot of work to do to get it ready?" Charlie's eyes swept over the grand staircase to the top of the middle landing. A thick black cloth hung over the frame of what Charlie assumed was a painting.

"I'm afraid so," Susan said. "My uncle Butch did the best he could, but you know he lived all by himself, and this place is huge. The whole inside is going to have to be remodeled I'm afraid, and my son and I are still going through all his stuff. I can't tell you how many trips we've already made to the dump."

Susan gestured toward the parlor on the right. Charlie stepped forward and a burst of cold air surrounded her, shimmying its way down her back. The skin on her bare arms broke into goosebumps and she shivered.

The parlor was in better shape. The walls and large carved mantle over the fireplace smelled of fresh paint and the wood floor, though scratched and worn, looked clean. Two elegant but contemporary cream-colored sofas flanked the mantle and Susan invited them to sit. Two large oil paintings hung on either side of the fireplace, a man and a woman, and their eyes followed her into the room.

"Who are they?" Charlie asked, pointing to the paintings.

"The gentleman is my ancestor, Willet Talmadge, and the lady is his wife, Eleanor Talmadge. They actually enlarged this house and made it grander in a time when most people had either lost their houses during the war or after because they couldn't afford to keep them any longer."

"How did he manage that?" Lisa sat next to Charlie and crossed her legs. She leaned forward and folded her hands in her lap. Susan took a seat on the sofa facing them.

"Well, I'm not a historian or anything, but he had a

large shipping company, and allegedly was a blockade runner during the war, which made him a fortune." Susan's hands fluttered around like birds caught in a trap and her eyes looked anywhere but at them.

"What about Aldus Talmadge?" Charlie kept her voice steady and calm, the same tone she would use when talking to an anxious customer. "Do you know much about him?"

Susan fidgeted and clasped her hands together, intertwining her fingers. "Just what everybody knows—that he was rumored to have raped and killed at least four girls—sharecropper's daughters who helped work the land owned by his father."

Another blast of cold air swirled around Charlie's shoulders, and from the corner of her eye, she caught movement in the foyer. Charlie's hands broke into a sweat and her heart sped up. Slowly she shifted her head just enough to see legs swinging back and forth, twisting. Her mouth tasted like ash.

"They hanged him? They hanged him in the house?" Charlie asked, her voice crescendoing. Lisa placed a hand on her shoulder.

"I—I don't think so," Susan said. She straightened her back and jutted her chin. "No. No, absolutely not."

"Charlie?" Lisa said softly. "You see something?"

Charlie closed her eyes for a few seconds and when

she reopened them, the legs were gone. She blew out a soft breath and shook her head.

"No. I—I thought I saw something, but it's gone now. It could be the house playing tricks." Charlie glanced toward Susan, offering a reassuring smile. Susan's face blanched and her dark brown eyes widened. "I'm sorry I didn't mean to scare you."

A nervous titter escaped Susan but her smile was only halfhearted. "You didn't. Trust me, I've experienced a lot of scares in this house already."

Charlie nodded and leaned forward with her elbows on her knees. "Can you tell me about the things that you've experienced?"

Susan cast her gaze to the floor and rubbed the back of her neck, pinching it hard with her bony fingers. "Well, of course, there's been inexplicable creaking noises, footsteps on the stairs. Things moving around in the attic. I had some papers go missing. And sometimes if I'm outside on the back porch, say around twilight, you know when things get dusky, I—" She stopped. Charlie exchanged a glance with Lisa and rose from her seat, moving to sit next to Susan.

Susan's nails dug into her palms and she whimpered softly. Charlie placed her hand on top of Susan's, trying to get her to relax her tight grip and an image flashed through her head. Susan standing in the cool night air, her arms wrapped around her waist, unable to look away from the dozen silvery orbs floating along the edge of the trees.

"It's all right, Susan," Charlie said softly. "I'm going to help you."

"My son thinks I'm crazy," Susan said, her voice shaking. "He even threatened to take me to MUSC to have me evaluated. He doesn't believe in any of this. He keeps telling me it's all in my head."

"It's always easy for someone to say when they don't have to live with it. Has he stayed here with you one night?"

"Oh, no, course not. He's too busy with his career."

"What does he do?" Lisa asked.

"He's a deputy sheriff."

"From my experience, the spirits don't really care whether he believes in them or not," Charlie said.

"We need to take a look around," Lisa said. "Will you be all right here by yourself?"

Susan glanced around the room. "Yes, I should be fine. Thank you. Thank you so much for believing in me. I was seriously beginning to think I was going crazy."

Charlie patted her shoulder. "No. Not crazy. There is definitely something going on with this property."

"Would it be weird for me to say thank God for that?" Susan said.

Lisa grinned. "Nope. Not at all."

* * *

CHARLIE WALKED AROUND THE EXTERIOR OF THE LARGE house ignoring the eyes from the woods trained on the back of her head. She knew at some point she would have to head over there and talk to them, find out who they were, what they wanted, and how they had come to be in this place. Even though Lisa was certain they were Aldus Talmadge's victims, Charlie was not quite so sure. They all looked to be dressed in clothes from different time periods. Maybe she would research missing girls over the past seventy or eighty years to see what came up.

As she made her way back around the corner of the house, a black Dodge Charger came barreling up the driveway spitting gravel and dust in its wake. It came to an abrupt halt right behind Lisa's BMW. A man got out of the car wearing a pair of khaki pants and a black polo with an embroidered insignia over his left breast pocket.

He looked directly at her with his mirrored sunglasses. "So you must be the psychic."

He took off his glasses, folded them up and stuck them in his pocket. He held out his hand and smiled, focusing his hazel eyes on her. The way his teeth gleamed it reminded her of an alligator with its mouth open. "I'm Jason Tate. I believe you're meeting with my mother today."

"Yes," Charlie said, not taking her gaze off of his hand.

She didn't want to touch him. She often saw things when she touched people—sometimes it drew out the spirits that had attached themselves or were looking out for the person. Sometimes it was their heart or their mind or a memory. It could have been any of those things with Jason Tate—and any one of them gave her a bad feeling. She didn't want to know what was in his mind or his heart or his memories, and she sure as hell didn't want to know about the spirits hanging around him. She forced herself to gaze up and smile, but left his hand dangling in the air. His fingers twitched and folded into a fist before he dropped it to his side.

"So, is my mother here?" He glanced up at the house.

"Yes, I believe she's inside. I was just looking around the property to see what we're working with."

His jaw clenched and his lips stretched into a smile but it never touched his eyes. "Great," he said. "So, have you figured it out?"

"Have I figured what out, exactly?"

His smile twisted into a grimace. "That this house isn't haunted. The things my mother experiences are all in her head."

"Maybe some of it can be explained logically, but there are definitely things on this property that defy logic."

"And that's your professional opinion?" His tone was

full of mockery. The energy pouring off him made it clear he was not happy that she was here.

"If you want to call it that, yes. It is." She crossed her arms and met his gaze. "I don't quite have a handle on it yet, but—" She glanced toward the woods. "When I'm done, your mother won't have a reason to be afraid anymore."

"My mother doesn't have a reason to be afraid now." He put his hands on his narrow hips and the muscles in his arms flexed. By his stance, he was a man used to using his authority to get his way, but Charlie refused to be bullied.

"I'm afraid I disagree with you on that. I don't think your mother's in any physical danger. At least I haven't sensed that—"

"Great—" he said. "Then she doesn't need you here, does she?"

"That's totally up to her. She may not be in immediate physical danger. but that doesn't mean the spirits living in this house and on this property can't do her harm."

He laughed, but it was a cold sound that sent a skittering chill across her skin. Stepping forward, he closed the gap between them and locked a heavy gaze on her. He was tall enough to make her crane her neck to look into his face and she didn't like the way her body reacted to the sharp cut of his jaw and his rugged handsomeness. She glared at him and took a step backward.

"I'm going to say this, and I want you to listen to me carefully," he said, lowering his voice. "I'm on to you. Do you understand? You are not the first *psychic* I've ever dealt with."

"Good," she said. "Then you know what to expect."

He made a scoffing noise, and a scowl twisted his mouth. "You know I take statements all the time from parents and grandparents, guardians, and foster parents whose kids have gone missing or run away. Every psychic I have ever known has been nothing but a fraud."

"I'm sorry that's been your experience. There are plenty of people out there who will take advantage of a situation. But I can assure you, the only thing I want to do is help your mother."

"Well, you better hope for your sake that's the truth because I'm gonna be watching you."

"You go right ahead. Watch away," she said, not backing down. "I have nothing to hide."

He glared at her, saying nothing.

"Jason?" Susan's sharp voice cut through their stare off. "What are you doing here?"

Jason broke his gaze finally, and he smiled. "Nothing, Mom. I just wanted to meet this psychic you hired. That's all. Make sure she understands what she's getting into."

Susan cocked her head and pressed her lips into a thin line. "Jason, you be good."

"Yes, ma'am," he said. "Can I talk to you please? Privately?"

"Charlie, I apologize if he's said anything to offend you. I'm afraid he's a little over-protective."

"Mom." He threw his hands up in the air. "I'm standing right here, quite capable of speaking for myself."

"Charlie, would you please excuse us?" Susan asked.

"Certainly." Charlie gave him a sideways glance and made her way up the porch, glad to be free of him. "I'll just go find Lisa."

"Thank you," Susan said sweetly. Charlie walked into the house out of earshot. She didn't want to hear the two of them argue. It was hard enough dealing with her own family issues; she certainly didn't want to intrude on theirs.

"Hey, there you are," Lisa said, descending the steps.

"What did you find?" Charlie asked.

Lisa shrugged one slim shoulder. "Well, the house looks like an episode of Hoarders. Lots of newspapers and stacks of boxes and rotting furniture. Rat droppings. Spiders. Palmetto bugs—dead and alive."

"Nice." Charlie's lips curled in disgust. "Anything else?"

"It's an old, creaky house. All the windows are drafty, and considering how close it is to the water and how hot the days and cool nights are this time of year—it could definitely account for some of the noises she hears."

"Did you feel any cold spots?"

Lisa shook her head. "No. Sorry. You?"

"No. Just the two I felt earlier. I did see the spirits of several girls at the edge of the woods."

"Did you go talk to them?"

"Not yet." Charlie glanced over her shoulder toward the front door. Susan's muffled voice rose. "I met the son."

"Yeah?" Lisa followed her cousin's gaze. "And?"

"He's definitely not a believer."

"Great. Do you think he's gonna be trouble?"

Charlie sighed, frowning. "Oh, yeah. Absolutely."

CHAPTER 5

Jason had watched from the kitchen as his mother entertained the psychic and her friend in the parlor. Psychics. What a bunch of hooey. Even though no one in the Sheriff's department would ever corroborate it, they had consulted psychics on occasion, usually at the request of grieving, desperate parents. All he had ever seen was a bunch of generalizations, guesses, and nonsense. Lots of "leads" that never once led to anything but heartache and frustration to both the parents and the sheriff's department.

But his mother was a believer. After his father left, she'd gone to a psychic-witch to get a love spell to get her husband back. It brought his father back, all right, but that was not a good thing, as far as Jason was concerned.

The only thing his father was good for was a smack across the mouth and taking money out of her wallet. When he left for the second time, Jason had to practically hold his mother down to keep her from going after him.

He'd noticed the psychic with the pale blonde hair and angelic face glancing at him and he stepped out of the doorway before his mother noticed.

He understood why his mother wanted this place to work. It was her last chance to really do something with her life. Sure, the house creaked and had cold spots and hot spots and sometimes he would see things from the corners of his eyes, but it was just his mind playing tricks. It sure as hell wasn't real. He just didn't know how to convince his mother of that, short of moving in here and proving it to her. If the place had decent Wi-Fi coverage he would have too, but right now his mother had other things to worry about besides running cable this far out. For some reason he couldn't explain, his phone battery kept dying out here too. That's what he got for choosing the crappy, free smartphone.

Finally, their chairs scraped across the wood floor and their footsteps head into the foyer. He listened as they said their goodbyes and the front door closed. He folded his arms and waited for his mother to come into the kitchen. She breezed past him, picking up her bag and slinging it over her shoulder.

"I know what you're gonna say, Jason, and I don't want to hear it," she said.

"Mom—" He leaned forward and scrubbed his chin between his thumb and forefinger. He had to choose his words carefully. "Just tell me why you feel this is necessary. Help me understand."

His mother didn't meet his eyes. "Because I don't feel safe here. Now, that's the last I want to hear about it."

Jason sighed and let his gaze drop to the floor. There was dirt ground into the dingy linoleum that would never come up no matter how much she scrubbed and a chunk of it was missing at the edge of the old Frigidaire. If she was going to make this into a bed-and-breakfast she was going to have to rip out this whole kitchen and put in a new one, but the wiring had to be done first.

"Mom, if you want to feel safe, get a security system or a dog. Anything but a psychic. I mean, where did you even find her?"

"You are too nosy for your own good." She sniffed and tipped her chin defensively. "And if you must know, she came highly recommended to me. By someone I personally know."

"Who?"

"My hairdresser."

"Oh, my lord." He dropped his face into his palm and shook his head. "Are you kidding me?"

"No, I am not kidding you. I completely trust this girl, and these are her cousins."

"Well, that's just fucking great."

"Jason David Tate! Your language reflects your character, and I raised you better than that."

His cheeks burned from being scolded like he was a little boy. He'd heard her philosophy on character his whole life and thought about it every time he opened his mouth and uttered a curse word.

"Yes, ma'am," he muttered. "Sorry." He folded his arms across his chest and met her eyes. "I just don't want to see you taken advantage of, that's all."

"I know, honey. I know." His mother stepped directly in front of him and pressed her hand against his cheek. "You have been my protector for a long, long time, and I appreciate it. I really do. But I know what I'm doing here. This place can be great. But we have to get rid of this... this..." She waved her hands in the air and her gaze shifted to the ceiling. "Bad energy before that can happen."

"And you're sure this girl can do that?"

"Yes. I'm certain of it. I have a good feeling about her. I've met a lot of psychics in my life, and she's the real deal. You just have to give her a chance." Her lips curved into a smile. Something crashed upstairs, followed by the sound of footsteps rushing down the grand staircase. His mother's wide, dark eyes fell on him and a shiver coursed through her thin frame. "Please tell me you heard that."

He took her hand in his and nodded. "I heard something, but more than likely it's just the sounds of an old house."

"I wish I knew how to convince you that you're wrong," she said.

"Sorry," he said, pulling his mother into his arms. She rested her head against his chest and they stood in the kitchen, not speaking for a moment. "Hey, Mom, is there any chance I can have the number to your hairdresser?"

"Jason, I'm not going to let you harass her." His mother pulled out of the embrace and frowned.

"I'm not going to harass her. I need a haircut and she does a good job with your hair."

"Jason," his mother said full of disbelief.

"What? I'm not kidding. I just want to get my hair cut. That's all."

"Fine," she said. "But I swear I will take you over my knee if you start hassling her. Do you understand me?"

He fought the urge to smirk. It was almost cute that his mother thought she could still take her thirty-two-year-old son over her knee. "Yes, ma'am."

Susan took her purse from the counter and pulled a pink card from her wallet. "If you mention my name, she'll give you ten percent off your first cut. She's very good, by the way. No one has done such a good job with my hair."

He studied the card, brushing his thumb over the embossed name— A Touch of Glamour Salon—Daphne Ferebee, Stylist and Owner. "I have no doubt about that."

CHAPTER 6

Raymond Kurtz wrapped his hands around the top of the push-broom handle and kept his head down, trying to ignore the voice in his head. Up until the other day, the only thing it had said to him was *don't drink*, over and over again. It soothed him at first, and reminded him of his mother—how she would rub her fat fingers over the cheap pink beads of her rosary. He'd even toyed with the idea that it was a prayer to that higher power they talked about at his meetings. But then the voice changed.

He moved the broom across the dingy linoleum flooring of Hare's Swifty Mart and Gas. Rounding the corner to the snack aisle, the voice started in on him again, making him look up.

Look at that skin. So beautiful. Don't you just want to reach out and touch it?

He shuddered internally, trying to keep his eyes on the trash and dirt accumulating in front of his broom. His eyes flitted to her back against his will. Her curly hair was pulled into loose ponytail and fell between her shoulder blades. The smooth, caramel-colored skin of her neck peeked from beneath her tight T-shirt. He licked his lips. What he wouldn't give for a beer.

She threw a glance over her shoulder at him. Her brow furrowed and her dark eyes glared at him.

Look at that face. Notice how the blood makes her throat pulse just a little. She wants you.

"What are you staring at?" she asked. Nope. No desire in that tone. His hands tightened on the broomstick and he continued pushing it forward.

Are you really going to let her get away with talking to you like that?

His shoulder twitched toward his ear and he kept his eyes down. Just one beer would make it all stop. Maybe he needed to call his sponsor again.

He got to the end of the row and started to turn the mop around but caught a glimpse of her reflection in the soda cooler. Her young breasts pushed against the dark, pink cotton and the skinny jeans she wore clung to every curve. Maybe the voice was right. How could she wear those clothes and not want some sort of attention?

That's right. That's exactly right. She wants it. Wants you. How would her skin taste?

Raymond wiped his mouth with the back of his hand. If he could just have a couple of beers, that stupid voice would shut up.

You don't need a drink, Ray. You just need to touch her. That's what will make all this go away.

"No," Ray said, startled by the sound of his voice.

"What did you say?" the girl asked.

Ray's eyes met her gaze. Her don't-mess-with-me stance made him take a step backward.

"Nothing," he mumbled.

She scowled at him, then went back to making her selection.

I can't believe you're going to let her get away with that! Coward! Ray shook his head and threw the mop handle onto the floor. He stormed past her, letting the back of his hand brush across her butt as he went.

"Hey!" She shot him a dirty look. "You better watch yourself."

"Sorry," he muttered. He stopped in front of the counter and stared at his co-worker Dave, sitting behind the register, flipping through one of the car magazines. "I gotta take a break now."

"It's not your time yet. Did you just throw that mop down? You can't leave it in the aisle like that. Somebody could trip."

"I have to take a break *now*." Ray scraped his short fingernails against the stiff denim of his jeans.

"Fine." Dave threw up his hands and his mouth twisted into a frown. "Take a break. So what if you've only been here an hour?" He folded his arms across his chest and tugged on his blue and orange vest, skewing his nametag.

Ray headed out through the back door, raking his hand through his thick, dark hair. He pulled his cell phone from his pocket and quickly maneuvered through his contacts. Cool evening air slapped him in the face and he took a few deep breaths. The briny scent of the marsh washed over him, soothing him. He opened his sponsor's contact and chose the option for call. His old fogey of a sponsor had a flip phone and barely knew how to make a call, much less text.

"Come on. Come on. Gene. Pick up. Pick up." He tapped his fingers against his thighs.

"Hi, you've reached Gene Hayes. I can't come to the phone right now but if you leave me a brief message and your number, I'll call you back soon as I can."

"Gene, it's Ray Kurtz," he said, unable to stop the desperation from creeping into his voice. "I need you, man. I want a drink so bad. I think if I don't have one soon something bad's gonna happen."

She walked across the side parking lot, catching his attention from the corner of his eye. The phone drifted away from his head and his breath sounded harsh in his ears. She strutted, shaking that heart-shaped behind of hers before stopping in front of a little red Chevy not even twenty feet from where he stood. Her keys jangled in her hand.

It wouldn't take much. Not much at all if he moved fast enough. Her sky-high heels put her at a disadvantage along with her small stature. If he struck her head first, there wouldn't be much of a fight.

Now, you're thinking. It would be even better if you could catch her around the throat. Squeeze a little of that attitude out of her. Just until she passed out. Her fate in your hands, quivering against you. You would own her and only you could decide to give her life or take it away.

His breathing grew longer and steadier. He could do this. Maybe if he did, the voice would just shut up and go away. Maybe. He found himself halfway across the gap between them before he remembered the cameras. He glanced up at the corner of the building, unsure of the lens's range for the side parking lot. He'd seen the monitors behind the counter and how clear the images were. The owner had even bragged about how good the video was when they were installed a couple of months ago. No. It was not a risk he could take. Not yet.

He watched her get hold of her key fob and press the unlock button. The car chirped two short times, and the headlights blinked. She glanced over her shoulder at him, her dark eyes narrowing with disgust. He took a step toward her. All the attitude she wielded before melted away and she rushed into the car, locking it with an audible click. Something bloomed inside his chest for the first time in his life, and his lips tugged into a smile.

You made her afraid of you. Fear is good. Fear is better than any drink you've ever imbibed. Just imagine how much more powerful it will feel when she's trembling beneath you.

"Power," he muttered, putting a name to the feeling filling his body. He put the phone to his ear again. "You know what, Gene? Never mind. I think I'm gonna be all right after all."

THE SUN SET LOW IN THE LATE-MARCH SKY AND THE YOUNG African-American girl stood up and stretched her back. She couldn't have been more than fourteen or fifteen but her clothes—a tattered brown skirt that skimmed the tops of her shoes and a muslin, sweat-stained blouse— made her appear older. She wore a muslin scarf tied around her head and wiped her forehead with the back of her hand.

Charlie wasn't sure exactly where she was, even though the surroundings seemed familiar. It had to be one of the islands, but the landscape didn't tell her which one. An eerie silence filled her senses. There were no sounds from the roads. It reminded her of her uncle Jack's place on John's Island late at night. The sounds of trucks and cars almost completely stopped that far out and the only sounds were those of a summer night, crickets, katydids, and frogs.

An expanse of freshly tilled earth stretched out in three directions, and she could see workers—mostly African-American—standing up like the girl nearby, finishing up their day from the look of it.

The girl looked in the basket near her feet and frowned. Charlie drew closer, surprised that the girl had not noticed her yet.

This is a dream.

Of course, maybe the girl was trying to show her something. Maybe if she closed her eyes and let herself drift into the girl's head she would know more.

When she opened her eyes, Charlie could see through the girl's eyes, hear her thoughts, and feel what she felt. Her name was Ruth Mathis and mainly what she felt was bone tired. At least until she saw the man approaching. Her daddy. He wiped his hands on his dusty overalls and pushed the wide brim of his soft felt hat up onto his head, revealing his dark weathered face.

"Ruthie?" he said, his tone full of weighty concern. He glanced at the long open trench she'd been tending. Disappointment deepened the lines around his mouth.

"You're not finished yet? Your mama will have supper on the table here soon."

Ruth bent over and picked up the basket for him to look. "Naw, sir, I still have another row to plant and cover."

"Girl," her father shook his head, frowning. "What am I gonna do with you? You begged me to come out to the fields to help with the planting, but you can't keep up. We're on a schedule. These taters have to be in the ground. Buzzy said the almanac is calling for rains to start in April. That's just a few days away. Now, if you can't keep up, I'm gonna have to send you back to the house to work with your mama."

"Please don't do that, Daddy," Ruth pleaded. "I can finish. There's still some daylight left. Please, Daddy, don't give up on me yet."

Her father scrubbed his rough chin and eyed his daughter. He held up one finger. "One chance, and it's all on you. You hear me, girl?"

"Yes, sir," Ruth said.

"All right, then," her daddy said. "You best get back to work. You don't want to be out this field in the dark."

"Naw, sir," Ruth said. She reached inside the basket and pulled a seed potato out and dropped it into the shallow. Her basket was still a third full of seed and she needed to hoe dirt to cover them once she finished the task. The others, her father and three brothers, had already finished their planting and were heading toward the road that ran along the back of the property. The sun dipped behind the trees. She picked up her basket and moved a little farther down the row.

"Ruth, you want me to stay with you and help you finish up?" her brother Hal asked. Hal was always looking out for her. Ruth glanced at her father, unable to ignore the look of disapproval.

"Naw, you go on, get outta here. I promised I'd do it all myself."

"You sure?"

"I'm sure. I just gotta get these two rows covered and I'll be along shortly."

"All right, then," he said. His wide, round eyes glanced around the field. "You be careful. Y'hear?"

"I will. Now go on." She shooed him away and headed toward the top of the row with her hoe to cover her seeds.

Twilight cast milky light over the field as she pulled dirt over the last shriveled-looking starter potato. The green shoot budding from the top was the only indication it was alive. She tamped the soil down lightly with the back of her hoe and stepped back to look at the ten rows she'd seeded today. Maybe she moved a little slower than her brothers, but it didn't mean she was destined to be confined to housework and cooking for the rest of her life. She picked up the hoe and headed for the dirt road leading home. The darkness fell faster than she expected, and even with the stars glowing above she had to rely partly on her memory.

The familiar clip-clopping of horse hooves came up behind her and she moved from the center of the road toward the side so the rider could pass. There was only one man she knew of who would be out this time of evening taking a ride—the youngest Talmadge boy. Although she supposed that at twenty he wasn't much of a boy anymore. Her grip tightened on the hoe resting on her shoulder. He was always polite enough but there was something about the way he stared, unblinking, as if he could see through her clothes. It always sent a shiver through her when she saw him. She stepped up her pace, hoping he would just pass her by. Her mama was probably close to having supper ready, and she hoped there would be hoecakes. Those were her favorite.

The horse moved up beside her, and his shadow loomed over her. "You're out late, aren't you, girl?"

"Yes, sir," she said, glancing sideways, trying to get a better look at him. From the length of his wavy hair, she knew it was him. Aldus Talmadge.

He made a *tsking* sound and gave his horse a light kick in the ribs. The horse sped up, and he yanked its reigns, making it turn sharply. The large, black beast came to a stop right in front of Ruth. It pawed at the gravel and snorted, making her take a step back.

"It's dangerous out here in the dark. Haven't you heard?" Aldus Talmadge said.

She had heard rumors about two other girls who had gone missing on other farms, but she hadn't paid it much mind. People came and went all the time, looking for something the land couldn't give them.

"Yes, sir," she said, side-stepping the horse. "I best get home. My mama and daddy are prob'ly worried by now."

He moved the horse forward, blocking her path. The beast champed at the bit, and made a low, warning rumble deep in its throat. "What's your name, girl?"

"My name is Ruth Mathis sir, now please let me pass." Her calm delivery masked the panic blooming inside her chest.

He pulled the horse's left rein, and the animal shifted its position out of Ruth's path. She kept her eyes straight forward trying to ignore the weight of his gaze as he watched her move beyond him. She shifted the hoe from her shoulder to her side before bolting forward into a run. Her boots crunched against the crushed gravel, competing with the horse's hooves grinding into the crushed gravel and sand of the dirt road behind her.

The rope went around her neck and yanked. For a moment, she was weightless, facing the indigo sky before landing hard on her back. All the breath rushed out of her body, and she struggled to breathe. He slipped off his horse and kicked the hoe she'd been holding out of her weakened grip.

He leaned over her, and even in the shadows she could see his cold, hard eyes staring at her, unwavering.

She clawed at her neck trying to loosen the noose, trying to breathe. He pulled tighter on the rope.

"That's it," he sneered. "You uppity little bitch."

She coughed and tried to turn on her side, but he pulled the rope tighter and put one knee on her leg. Panic ripped through her body when she realized he wanted her to be afraid. Wanted her helpless and scared and compliant. She gritted her teeth. No matter how powerful he was, she refused to go down without a fight. She struck out, aiming for his face, her fingernails raking across his cheek, drawing blood.

The force of the blow made her vision go dark before white and blue stars blinded her for a moment. He uttered profanities at her for her impudence. Something hot and wet landed on her cheek. The splatter landed in her eye, stinging. She wiped away his stinking, mucus-y spit from her face. He stood up and yanked hard on the rope again. It tightened and lifted her from the ground. Her nails broke to the quick on the thick coil of sisal. She choked, gasping for any little bit of air she could get. The world darkened at the corners of her eyes before everything went black.

* * *

THE FEEL OF COOL, SANDY DIRT HITTING RUTHIE'S FACE
brought her around again. How long had she been out?
The darkness pressed in on her and she knew her mama
must be worried sick by now. She tried to move, but
sharp, burning pain shot through the bottom half of her
body. What had he done to her? Another shovel full of
dirt struck her in the face choking her. She wiped at her
eyes, searching the darkness for the source. The sheer
black stretched up what seemed a long way. Trees swayed
far above her, and moonlight flickered through the leaves
in places. She was in the woods. She sometimes thought
she heard crying coming from the thick growth of trees
on her way to the fields in the early dawn of morning—
but she refused to look, in case she saw a haint looking
back at her.

Another shovel full of dirt rained down on her legs
this time. His tall broad silhouette loomed above and she
thought for a moment he was no man, but the devil
himself, and he meant to bury her alive.

"Please," she tried to speak, but all that came out was
a squeak. "Please, sir, don't do this. I promise I won't tell
nobody."

"You're right about that," he said and heaped more
dirt on her.

With no choices left, she screamed through the

rawness—better to have a sore throat than to be dead. Maybe someone would hear. Maybe her daddy was out looking for her by now. Maybe. He jumped into the hole with her and raised his shovel—Ruth raised her arm to shield herself but flat metal came down hard. Once. Twice. The world swam in grays and blacks. Her mama wouldn't know what happened to her. Her mama—

CHAPTER 7

Charlie jerked awake, sweating and chilled at the same time. Her hand flew to her neck and head, feeling around, making sure there was no injury. She pushed up on her elbow and glanced around the room. This was her room, and she was alone. It was just a dream. Just a horrible dream.

She glanced at the clock on her bedside table. The bright red numbers read 12:10 a.m. She picked up her cell phone and clicked on the text icon. She hesitated for a moment. Would he be up? Would he even answer her? Their history suggested no. But her heart hoped. Her thumbs began to move across the flat keyboard on her smart phone.

Are you awake?

Charlie stared at the screen waiting for the three dots. A

few seconds later, the phone buzzed in her hand and she
yelped, dropping it on her belly. Scott's picture appeared. It
was one of her favorites of him and Evan at Edisto Beach
the last summer before things fell apart. He was grinning,
holding up a fish that Evan had caught in the surf, so proud.

"Hello?" she answered.

"You okay?" Scott asked. She could hear gravel in his
voice. She had woken him up.

"I had a bad dream."

He grew quiet, then he sighed softly. "Do you want to
tell me about it?"

"No," she said. "It will just piss you off."

"Why did you call me, then?"

She chuckled. "I didn't. You called me. I texted you."

"Oh, right," he said, sounding sleepy. "Why don't you
try me?"

"It's just about this woman, girl, really. On this case
I'm working on."

"Case? What sort of case?" Concern edged into his
voice.

She felt almost embarrassed to tell him. "It's this
thing Daphne asked me to help with."

"Your cousin Daphne? Your flaky cousin Daphne?"
He emphasized the word flaky, and an irritation flashed
through her.

"Daphne is not flaky. She's actually quite successful."

"Right. Sorry. Successful flaky cousin Daphne."

"She has her own business, and a very successful haircare vlog."

"Of course, she does. So, what exactly does she have you doing?"

"Promise you won't be mad, and no laughing at me."

"By legal decree, I don't think I'm allowed either of those things anymore," he said, sounding sad. When it was all said and done, both of their hearts had been broken, not just hers. She had to do a better job of remembering that.

"We're investigating a haunted house." The line grew quiet. Too quiet. "You still there?"

"Yeah. I'm still here," he grumbled.

"You're mad," she said softly.

"No, I'm not." The line crackled, and she thought he was rubbing his face with his hand. "It's just—"

"Just what?" She already knew the answer and couldn't blame him for it.

"I divorced you so I wouldn't be woken up in the middle the night because of some dream you had."

"You and I both know that's not why we divorced. It would make you really shallow if it was." She took a deep breath and continued. "You divorced me because you didn't know how to make me happy, and you tried really, really hard for a really long time."

He sighed in her ear. "I still don't know how to make you happy, Charlie."

She shrugged. "It was never your job."

"Char—why are you calling me?"

"I didn't, remember?" she teased.

"Fine. Why did you text me, then?"

She raked her fingers through her hair, trying to find an answer. "Because I wanted to feel safe for a minute."

"The dream made you feel unsafe? I've never known you to be afraid of a ghost, Charlie."

"You say that as if you believe in them."

"No—I say that as if *you* believe in them," he corrected. "Is this thing you're doing dangerous? Should I be worried about your safety?" The real concern in his voice touched her.

"Not physically. We'll have to see about spiritually and emotionally."

"Be careful. Okay? Please? I have no right to ask for me, but I do for Evan."

His request sent a pang of sadness through her. He was worried she might hurt herself again. She had caused so much pain to this man and even though he couldn't live with her, couldn't believe in her the way she needed, he would always love her.

She blew out a soft breath. "How is Evan?"

"He's good. He has big math test tomorrow, and he's really looking forward to your weekend together."

"Me too. Give him a kiss for me, okay?"

"I will. Good night, Char."

"Good night, Scott, and thank you—for listening."
She pressed the red phone button on her screen, ending
the call.

A chill skittered over her shoulders and she shivered.
There was no form, but the chill was enough for her to
recognize an unwelcome spirit. She reached for the stone
pendant hanging around her neck and brushed her
thumb over it. Closing her eyes, she whispered over and
over, "You are not welcome here. This is my safe space.
You need to leave."

A moment later, the air in the room felt more
breathable and peaceful. After she was sure it was gone,
she laid back down with the pendant still between her
thumb and forefinger—ready to ward off any more
spirits, even in her dreams.

CHAPTER 8

The main street of Palmetto Point was lined
with parking spaces for the businesses Jason
passed on his way to A Touch of Glamour
Salon. He slowed the car and read the signs: Duguid's
Pharmacy, the Kitchen Witch Café, a couple of boutique
shops that sold women's clothing, Pralines 'n Dreams
candy store, Condon's Mercantile and Hardware,
Chalmers Antiques, Twice as Good Consignments, Hill's
Ice Creamery and Maudie's Seafood Restaurant, before
finally seeing the pink orchid-shaped sign for the salon.
At that time of day, there wasn't much competition for
parking and he pulled into one of the spots in front of the
salon.

Through the large front window, he could see only
one stylist still working. She was short and slim and had

74

chin-length dark brown hair. A bell jingled above his head as he pushed open the door and she glanced at him. Her large blue eyes matched the blue streaks of hair framing her face. She barely looked old enough to drive much less work as a stylist in a successful hair salon.

"Jason?" she chirped, smiling wide.

"Yep, that's me." He shoved his hands into the pockets of his jeans.

"I'll be with you in just a few minutes. Can I get you something to drink while you wait? I've got water, soda, and wine. Pick your poison."

"Thanks, but I'm good." He wondered if she had a license to serve liquor on the premises, and made a mental note to check.

"Okay, well, you're welcome to take a seat here." She pointed to the chair next to the one where she was working. "Or you can sit in the waiting area. There are plenty of magazines to look through if you'd like."

"Thanks," he said. He took a seat in one of the white leather chairs in the waiting area. Picking up one of the magazines from the modern acrylic coffee table he pretended to read while appraising the long room. It all looked like something out of an upscale magazine. She must have been doing pretty well since her name was on the sign. Maybe he would check her financials, as well. See if there was anything shady going on.

He watched as she painted some sort of colored goop

onto thin strands of the girl's hair. She stepped back a moment and chewed on the sharp tip of the brush in her hand, surveying her work. She picked up one more bit of hair and painted a little more goop on it before abruptly disappearing behind a freestanding wall made of reclaimed wood. A moment later, she rolled out a tall contraption with long, bendable arms that had lamps attached. She plugged in the unit, pushed it close to her client and arranged the lamps so the pink bulbs inside shined on the woman's head.

Daphne pivoted toward him and smiled. "Your turn."

Jason rose from the waiting area and took a seat in the chair next to the woman being baked by the pink lights. "This place is pretty fancy for Palmetto Point."

Daphne grinned and wrapped a black protective cape around him, fastening it snuggly at his neck. "Not really. We have a ton of wealthy retirees in this area. They expect upscale, and this way they don't have to drive all the way to Charleston to get it."

"Oh," he said. "I didn't realize. I thought this was more of a tourist town."

"We have those too," she said, combing through his shaggy mane with her fingers. "So, what would you like me to do today? Keep the same but make it shorter and clean it up? Or are you looking for a new style?"

An unexpected anxiety flooded his belly at the mention of a new style and he wrapped his fingers around the chrome arm of the chair and squeezed. "Short and clean is good." He forced a smile. "I have a pretty conservative job, so a new style would be kinda risky."

"Okey-dokey, shorter it is then." She gave him a reassuring smile. "So, what you do you that makes a new hairstyle such a risky proposition?"

"I'm a deputy sheriff."

"Oooh, my cousin Lisa's boyfriend is a deputy too. Maybe you know him. Billy Manges?"

"I know of him. I think he's contracted directly by Palmetto Point through the sheriff's department, so we don't really cross paths."

"Huh. That makes sense. Let's get your hair washed." She touched his shoulder, prompting him to stand up. "You must see a lot of interesting things."

She led him behind the freestanding wall to a separate area with three dark gray sinks and white chairs that matched the ones up front. He took a seat and leaned back against the sink and she wet his hair. The feel of the warm water and the way she lathered up his hair and scrubbed his scalp relaxed him. There was more strength in her hands than he expected. When she was finished shampooing and conditioning his hair, she wrapped it in a towel, squeezing most of the wetness out.

"Ready?"

"Sure," he said, wondering if she always sounded like a happy princess in a fairytale. She led him back to the stylist chair. She guided his head forward until his chin hit his chest. "So, Daphne," he said, watching as the first locks of his hair began to fall to the floor. "How long have you lived in Palmetto Point?"

"Pretty much my whole life," she said. The scissors felt cold against the skin of his neck. "What about you? Did you grow up here?"

"No. I actually grew up in Charlotte. But I've got family here. I used to come visit my great uncle when I was a kid and really fell in love with the area, so I moved here after college and joined the sheriff's department."

"Nice." She shifted his head to the right, but made him keep his gaze down. "My cousin Jen used to live in San Francisco, but she came back after she got pregnant, and my cousin Lisa lived in Columbia for a while, but she hated being away from the water. So she came back too. I've never lived anywhere but here. Can't imagine living anywhere else."

"Yeah," he said. "My mom really speaks highly of you. Said you are great at what you do."

"I just love your mother. She is the sweetest lady. I'm so sorry that she's having such problems with her new house." He could hear the smile in her voice.

"Yeah," he said. "She's hired some psychic to come and take a look."

"Oh, yeah!" Daphne said. "That's my cousin Charlie."

"You sure have a lot of cousins," he teased.

Daphne snorted. "Yeah. We all grew up together. And Charlie's great. I have no doubt she'll be able to take care of it for your mom. She means the world to me as a customer, and I just hate that she's so scared."

"So, you really believe in this stuff? Ghosts, I mean."

"Sure," she said. "This is one of the most haunted areas in the whole United States. I actually grew up in a haunted house. It was my cousin Charlie who helped the ghost move on."

"How did she do that?"

Daphne leaned in close and gently pulled his ear down to get at the surrounding hair. "She talked to it. It didn't want to go at first, but with a little coaxing it finally left. I actually kind of missed it after it was gone."

"So, that's what she's going to do for my mom?" He threw a glance over at the young woman sitting next to him. Her thumbs moved rapidly over the screen of her phone, texting someone. He lowered his voice, feeling weird about talking about this subject at all. "She's gonna just talk to it?"

"Well, yeah, to start with. There's some other stuff she can do too. Burn some sage. Make a salt circle around the house. I think they met with your mom yesterday, but I haven't heard how it went. Have you talked to your mom?"

"Uh—yeah, she did mention something. She seemed to really like her."

"Excellent. My cousins are very likable—well, Charlie is, anyway. Lisa can be a little brusque, but once you get past that crabby exterior, she's really lovable." Daphne chuckled to herself and muttered, "Sometimes."

"So, y'all don't get along very well?"

"No, we get along fine. You just have to understand, we're more like sisters than cousins. Lisa's the oldest and I'm the baby, so—"

"I see. So, there's contention. What about Charlie? Where does Charlie fit in?"

"Charlie is totally a middle child. You know the one that never gets any attention and just wants everybody to get along."

"Hmm, so does she do this kind of thing for a living?"

"Charlie? No, not at all. I had to practically beg her. She's a rep for a local call center. Although she does do psychic readings sometimes. I even made her a website and a Facebook page, but she doesn't do anything with them, really. I keep telling her if she would just advertise, she could totally quit her job."

"She's that good, huh?" He started to nod but Daphne held tight to his head.

"Careful, wouldn't want to accidentally snip your ear off." She smiled at him in the mirror.

"No, we definitely don't want that. Sorry." His lips tugged into a half-smile. "So, Charlie's that good, huh?"

Daphne continued to cut his hair. "Yeah, Charlie's the best I've ever seen."

"You've seen a lot of psychics?" Jason said. He cringed internally at his derisive tone. It wasn't the way to get someone to talk, and he knew it.

Daphne grew quiet for a moment bringing his head up straight as she combed through his dark, damp hair, checking her work. "You have really healthy hair. I can already tell you work out. You must eat right too."

"Thanks," he said. "I try. So, you know a lot of psychics?"

"You sure are inquisitive." Daphne laughed, but it sounded hollow and nervous. She stepped back and met his gaze in the mirror.

"I don't mean to pry."

Daphne's brow furrowed and her ever-present smile faded. "You know, I think you do, actually."

"Uh. Pardon me?"

"Why are you really here?"

"I needed a haircut. My mom recommended you. She even said you'd give me ten percent off for mentioning her." He held her gaze in the mirror, letting his lips stretch into a wider, reassuring grin.

Daphne narrowed her eyes. "So, that's your story, huh?"

"There's no story." The muscles in his cheeks cramped from holding the grin.

Daphne glanced toward her other client. The young woman was too engrossed in her phone to notice them, though. Daphne stepped closer and ran her hand through his drying hair, finger styling it. "You don't know this about me, but I'm a sensitive too. Just like Charlie. I'm not quite as attuned to the other side as she is, but we both have one thing in common. The ability to know when someone's lying."

"That's a handy skill to have." Jason's smile faded. "What other skills do you have?"

"Me? Well, I'm really good at making people feel good about themselves and seeing what someone wants even when they may not know what it is."

"Hmmm," he said. "That just means you can easily take advantage of somebody."

"Sure. If I were an evil witch, but my mother raised me better than that. What about yours?"

"My mother? She did a great job."

"Good, glad to hear it." She held his gaze a moment longer. "We should get you dry and on your way."

Daphne pulled the hairdryer from the chrome cart holding her tools and with the flip of a switch, she ended the conversation.

CHAPTER 9

J ason Tate dropped back two car lengths to ensure that Charlie didn't notice him following her. On the seat next to him lay a file folder with all the information he'd managed to gather: driving record (no speeding tickets in the last three years), financial records (credit card bills paid off monthly—who does that?), divorce decree and custody agreement. On paper, she was the perfect citizen. With one exception, her divorce from Scott Carver. Somehow in the great state of South Carolina, Ms. Charlotte Grace Payne had lost custody of her ten-year-old son to her ex. A rarity in his experience working with the courts. Sure, Carver was a doctor, from a well-to-do family, but what had she done not to at least have joint custody? He had an appointment with her ex-husband later, and he couldn't wait to bring it up. Maybe their parting was not so amicable. Maybe, just maybe, the good doctor would give him the dirt he needed. He could hope, anyway.

The blinker of her blue Honda Civic came on, signaling her lane change and one of her brake lights flickered and burned out.

Jason fought the urge to flip on his lights and pull her over but he thought better of it. It was too soon to let her know he was following her.

He shadowed her on Highway-17 heading toward downtown Charleston. She zipped across the Ashley River Bridge to the Lockwood exit and it became harder not to be noticed once she turned from Lockwood on to Calhoun Street. He kept one car length between them for as long as he could. Where was she going? Finally, she turned into a parking garage off George Street and he followed her in, not wanting to lose sight of her.

He parked and waited for her to pass his car before he got out and began to follow her three blocks to Charleston College's library.

The early afternoon sun glinted off her pale, blonde hair and she walked with a little bounce in her step. No mom jeans for her—she wore skinny jeans and a form-fitting, red T-shirt. It was hard to admit, and he'd deny it if someone asked, but he *did* find her attractive, which made him even more determined to find something on her. Surely, something dark lurked behind that angelic face.

She crossed the street, and he followed her into the library. She approached the circulation desk and spoke to one of the librarians for several minutes. He ducked into the coffee shop off the main lobby. A small table hidden behind one of the large pillars, gave him a good view of her but allowed him to remain out of her line of sight.

The tall, balding man behind the desk kept flicking his eyes from her face to her chest, which made Jason uncomfortable. Finally, he nodded and wrote something down for her. A wide smile crossed her face, and she headed toward the right corner of the building, disappearing into a stairwell. Jason scowled. There was no way she wouldn't notice him now, but maybe he could make that work in his favor.

FINDING OLD NEWSPAPER ARTICLES FROM THE *POST AND Courier* without an exact date turned out to be more difficult than Charlie had thought. Most of it had been put onto microfiche. But there were dates missing because of the merger of the *Charleston Daily News* and *The Evening Post*. There were copies of *Charleston Daily News* going all the way back to 1863, but only selected dates. Charlie scanned through every article she could find, making notes in a small, wire-bound notebook she'd brought. There were no articles about missing girls on Talmadge Island, but there was a short article on Aldus Talmadge's death. The paper stated that after Talmadge had been formally charged with the rape and murder of one Amelia Hannagan, a local farmer's daughter, Talmadge had somehow escaped captivity, only to be found hanging by his neck in the foyer of his parents' home. Charlie put the heels of her hands over her eyes and rubbed them and the scene played out in her mind—Talmadge escaping, going home to his mother, only to be handed over to an angry mob by her.

"Mother? Mother! Help me!" Talmadge screamed. One of the men slipped a noose around Talmadge's neck while another one held him down.

"No one can help you now, Aldus. Lord knows I've tried, but you have brought such shame upon us. May God forgive you, because I cannot." The old woman turned into the parlor, closing the ornate double-doors behind her.

Talmadge's screams echoed through her head across time. No justice had been served by hanging him this way, especially not for the girls he'd killed, whose names weren't known. Charlie shook her head trying to rid herself of the image of them all, standing at the edge of those woods, looking to her for some sort of atonement that she wasn't sure even existed.

"Ms. Payne? It's Ms. Payne, right?" a voice said from behind.

Charlie turned and found Jason Tate standing behind her in full uniform. Her gaze flitted to the gun holster on his hip then back to his face. His lips curved into a smile, but it looked as if it pained him to wear it. His dislike for her came off him in waves, and she wondered if he was even aware of it.

"Doing a little research?"

"You could say that."

"Any luck finding something that will help you completely defraud my mother?"

Charlie gritted her teeth to keep from saying something she might regret. He was just not going to let it go, was he? "What brings you here?" she finally asked, raising her voice. The person two stalls over glared at her.

"I'm doing a little research myself," he said.

"Really?"

"Yep."

"I thought you were some sort of hotshot deputy sheriff or something. Shouldn't you be out deputy-sheriffing? Surely, there are present-day crimes that need solving."

"Don't worry about me, honey. I just wanted to remind you that I'm watching you."

"Yeah, you made it clear before, Deputy." Charlie emphasized the last word. "And I made it clear that you're not going to find anything. So, why keep threatening me?"

"It's not a threat. You scam my mother, I will arrest you all. Do you understand me?"

"No one is trying to scam your mother. All I want to do is help. I would have thought that you of all people would want that."

"My mother has an over-active imagination. She doesn't need a psychic. What she needs is a—" He bit back the rest of his sentence.

The word popped into her head. "She needs a shrink? That's what you were going to say, right?"

Jason's face flushed and his brows drew together into a heavy line above his eyes. His jaw clenched and nostrils flared. "Obviously, you're really good at mind games."

Charlie sighed. "This isn't a game, and the fact that you don't realize that makes me even more terrified for your mother. I don't care if you believe in me or not but you need to believe in her. Her fear is real."

"I didn't say it wasn't," he started.

"Yes, you did. The minute you thought it could be solved with a trip to a psychiatrist. You want to help her? Stop projecting your ideas of how things should be—how *she* should be—and start supporting her how she is now, including her fears. All she wants is for you to believe in her. That's all anybody wants, really. Someone to believe in them." Charlie glanced at her phone and flipped off the microfiche machine. She removed the sheet of fiche and stood up. "Now, if you'll excuse me, I have to get to work."

Charlie slung her purse strap over her shoulder and walked away, refusing to give him the satisfaction of looking back at him.

* * *

"What do you mean Jason Tate was there? What was he doing there?" Lisa asked, sounding irritated. Charlie balanced her cell phone on one leg as she drove.

"I don't know what he was doing there exactly, other than trying to be menacing to me. He told me he would arrest me if I was trying to scam his mother."

"Did he?" Lisa fumed. "I'd like to see him try."

"It's probably better if we play nice. I don't need any sort of trouble. I'm just not sure where to go next. I thought for sure there would be something more in the papers."

"I've been thinking about that. As much as I hate to admit this out loud—I can't imagine any paper around here reporting on missing African-American girls. Not before the forties or fifties, anyway."

"Yeah, unfortunately, I had that thought too," Charlie said.

"Maybe we should check with some of the museums.

I mean who's gonna know the history better than a historian at a museum? Maybe they can tap resources that we can't."

"You know, there's an agricultural museum in Palmetto Point. I mean, I know it's not on the same island but—" Charlie said.

"Yeah, but it's agriculture, which is pretty central to the area. There's also a maritime museum. They may know more about Talmadge's shipping company. That's originally how they made their money."

"All right. I've got to get to work, but that gives me some place to look." Charlie turned into the parking lot of her call center.

"Let me know what you find."

"I will." Charlie had her eye out for a parking space.

"Oh, and if he keeps harassing you, just let me know. I have no problem opening a complaint against him with his superiors," Lisa said.

Charlie chuckled, but felt grateful for her cousin's protectiveness. "Yeah—I know you don't."

CHAPTER 10

Daniela wandered around the aisles of the small convenience store, sometimes running her fingers over the merchandise. She stopped a moment to admire the little rhinestones glued to her fake blue and gold nails. She liked the way they glinted, even in this light. Her aunt had given her hell over them and screamed at her for wasting her lunch money on such trivial things. But they were so pretty, and she never ate lunch, anyway. So, why shouldn't she spend the money on something she really wanted?

On her third pass around the store, she noticed him watching her. He just stood in the corner holding the handle of the push mop, his eyes following her every move. He was older, and he wasn't bad looking, except for the way he gazed at her, as if he might be picturing her naked, creeped her out. If he didn't stop she would say something to the other attendant sitting behind the counter flipping through some magazine.

A nervous knot tightened in her belly when he started to follow her from aisle to aisle. Maybe she should just go home. Forget about the stupid argument with her aunt. It just made her so mad that her aunt didn't understand that the world was different today. She may have only been fifteen years old and the last of her friends to lose her virginity, but that was only technical. She'd done almost everything else.

She glanced at the clock over the beer coolers. Its red digital numbers glowed 11:39. Her boyfriend was late. He was supposed to meet her at 11:30. She pulled out her phone, whipped off a quick text and waited for him to reply. She stopped in front of the candy bars, glancing toward the attendant behind the counter. He clearly wasn't paying any attention to her. Looking left toward the other one, with the dry mop, she found him standing at the end of the candy aisle leering at her, nodding to himself, as if he was listening to someone. His thick lips twisted into a smirk and his eyes met hers. He started pushing the mop again.

"Take it," he whispered as he passed her. A gust of cold air blew across the back of her neck and shoulders sending a chill down her spine. She looked up at the ceiling. Maybe she was standing under an AC vent. The hair on her arms stood at attention when she noticed the only vents were in the four corners of the store. Slowly she brought her gaze back to the candy, trying to ignore him. It wouldn't take much to just slip a couple of Snickers bars into her purse. Still, in her head she could hear her aunt's voice scolding her—*Stealing is a sin. Do you really want to go to hell over a couple of candy bars?* Daniela sighed and took a step back from the candy. She didn't want to wait inside anymore under creepy guy's gaze. She turned and headed out the door to wait for her boyfriend.

CHARLIE COULD FEEL HIS LUST FOR THE GIRL ALMOST AS clearly as if the feelings were her own. He kept pushing the wide, dirty dust mop past her. The girl's cloying perfume coated the back of his throat with each pass. Such a pretty, young girl didn't need to smell like a two-bit hooker. Didn't she know that? He pictured himself cupping her small firm breasts.

His thoughts made Charlie's stomach churn and if this weren't a dream, she might have vomited. When he followed her outside, Charlie couldn't seem to pass through the glass door. She wrapped her hands around the metal handle and rattled it back and fort,h but the door wouldn't budge. Locked in. She cursed under her breath, watching helplessly as he sidled up next to her, attempting to make conversation with her.

"Come on," Charlie said under her breath. "Come back inside where it's safe."

"She won't, you know?" a voice said. Charlie shifted her gaze from the girl to the man standing beside her. All the saliva in her mouth turned to dust when she met his black eyes.

"You," she said, recognizing him immediately from the vision she'd had in the library.

"You." He smirked and something about it made her so angry she wanted to slap him.

"You're Aldus Talmadge," she said.

"You have me at a disadvantage." Charm oozed from his voice and his dark gaze focused fully on her face. "You know my name, but I don't know yours. You came to my house, but we weren't properly introduced. I must remember to scold my niece for being remiss in her duties as hostess."

Charlie's jaw tightened. "Your niece," she started, "didn't introduce us, because you're dead. The real question is, why are you still hanging around?"

His lips stretched first into a grin, then continued,

becoming a grotesque leer that made Charlie's skin crawl. He stepped closer. "I am hanging around, as you say, because my work isn't done yet. See?"

His gaze shifted toward the glass door and Charlie instinctively followed his lead. The walkway where the girl had stood only moments before was empty. Red taillights glowed in the distance, and the white truck turned right, speeding off, tires squealing.

"They belong to me now."

A burst of fury exploded in her chest and she struck out, aiming for his face. He caught her by the wrist and the sound of his laugh chilled her to her soul. *But how could that be? He's a ghost,* her mind cried. He was more solid than any ghost she had ever seen—but of course this was a dream. He wasn't real. None of this was real.

"Get your hands off me," she said, shaking out of his grip.

"You are a spirited thing, aren't you? And so pretty." He lifted his hand to brush it across her cheek and she recoiled.

Never in her life had she felt the need to spit on someone. It was unlady-like and hateful, her grandmother—God rest her soul— would have not only been disgusted, she would have been disappointed. Something Charlie had spent most of her youth avoiding. But this man. This ghost. This ghost-man infuriated her beyond any fury she had known before, and she couldn't stop herself from hocking as much saliva as she could muster toward his pale, refined face.

The sound of his laughter shocked her, and she stepped back, watching as he pulled a fine, silk handkerchief from a pocket. He wiped away the glistening spittle coating his cheek. "Oh, I can't wait to break you."

"Break me?" Charlie's mouth twisted into a grimace and her stomach wrenched with revulsion. "You will never get the chance."

"We shall see about that." He grinned and took a step back. With each step, he faded until finally he disappeared near the soda cooler.

Charlie glanced at the attendant behind the counter. He didn't look up. Her eyes scanned the space above the counter, spotting the cameras positioned mounted near the ceiling—two in each corner and one right above the checkout.

Stepping outside the building, the cool evening air washed over her. It was just a gas station on a darkened road with no real landmarks to guide her. The only thing that stood out to her was the turtle and hare logo in the center sign above each gas pump. She stepped off the curb to get a better look at the sign. Maybe if she could remember it when she woke up, she could find the place.

Maybe none of this had happened yet. Maybe there was still time to stop it.

Something tightened around her throat when her foot touched the pavement of the parking lot, and her hands flew toward her neck. A thick coil of sisal rope scraped against her fingertips. She scratched at it, drawing blood.

His voice snaked through her head, silky and deadly. *We shall see.*

She struggled to breathe, and the noose tightened. Her vision darkened around the edges. She couldn't pass out, not here, not before she could tell someone. Not yet—

CHARLIE SAT UP STRAIGHT IN BED, COUGHING AND GASPING for air. She half-expected to see him standing at the end of her bed, his dark coal eyes burning with hatred and lust, but the room was empty. She let out a deep sigh and buried her face in her hands. She had told him he could not break her, but sitting here in the darkness, trying to shake the feel of the rope around her neck, she wasn't so sure.

She picked up her phone and scrolled through her contacts. Texting Scott was out. She'd already used her quota of calls with him this week, and with an Evan weekend coming up, she couldn't chance Scott thinking twice about him spending time with her. If Scott believed for one moment that she was unstable, he would move heaven and earth to keep her son from her. No, she couldn't have that; she only saw Evan every other weekend and two Wednesdays a month. Since soccer started her time with her son had seriously been cut.

Thumbing past Daphne's and Jen's numbers, she landed on Lisa's contact info. Lisa was the most pragmatic. She would be able to punch holes through this dream. She pressed the text option and quickly typed her message.

He was in my dream. Please call me.

Less than fifteen seconds later, the phone rang in her hand.

"Tell me. What happened?" Lisa said, her voice full of gravel.

"I'm sorry I shouldn't have—"

"Of course, you should have. Now, tell me what happened?"

Charlie recounted the dream down to the last painful detail. When she was done, there was only silence on the line. Had Lisa fallen back asleep? She couldn't blame her if she had. It was two-thirty a.m.

Finally, Lisa said, "I need you to do something for me."

"Of course, what?"

"Do you have a box of salt?"

"Salt? Yes, of course." Charlie knew where Lisa was going with her suggestion.

"Good. I need you to go into your kitchen and get it. Then I want you to put a ring of salt all the way around your bed."

"Do you think for one minute that's really going to stop him?"

"Yes, I do. And if you think long and hard enough, you do too. You need to protect yourself. It's the simplest, easiest line of defense until we can talk to Jen."

"What about the girl? She was real. I know it."

"Maybe she was, maybe she wasn't. Right now, there's not much you can do about it."

"What if he is somehow influencing this man to take girls? We have to stop him."

"I agree, and we will, but for now, for my peace of mind, please go get the salt."

"Lisa—it was just a dream. He can't really hurt me physically."

"You woke up because you couldn't breathe, right? In my book, that's hurting you."

"Damn him," Charlie said under her breath. "I feel like he's winning already."

"He can only win if he kills you. So, go get the damn salt and put it around your bed." Lisa was used to giving orders and having them followed.

"You know, Daphne's right about you. You are very bossy."

"Yes, I am. Especially when it comes to protecting the people I love. Now, don't make me get up in the middle the night and come over there. Because you know I will."

"Yes. I do know." Charlie smiled, glad that she wasn't alone in the world. "Thanks for listening to me and believing me."

"Why wouldn't I?" Lisa asked matter-of-factly. "You gonna be all right?"

"Yeah. I think so." Charlie pushed the covers off and threw her legs over the side of the bed. She walked through the darkened apartment with the phone in her hand. "I'll call you tomorrow."

Charlie ended the call and placed the phone on the kitchen counter. The moon shone in through the kitchen windows casting a white glow across the vinyl flooring. She opened the cabinet and grabbed the box of iodized salt from the first shelf. Her heart thudded its way up her throat. His black eyes stared out at her, reflected in the glass of the cabinet door. Her whole body went cold as he rushed toward her, moving through her, dropping the temperature around her enough that her breath puffed out in a cloud. His dark shadow appeared, not quite solid. Her hands shook as she flipped open the top of the salt and poured a handful into her palm. She flung it out toward the shadow. "Get out of my house! You are not welcome here. Get out. Get out! Get out!"

The shadow screeched and dissipated. As she poured a line of salt in front of her back door, she could have sworn she heard him chanting her name in a whisper.

CHAPTER 11

Sugar adjusted her beach towel over her bent arm and slipped on her flip-flops. She closed the door to her little apartment behind her and locked it, dropping the key on its long string into her beach bag. There were no beaches at Summerfield Retirement Community, but there was a pool and she loved to swim.

"Well, good morning, Sugar," Dick Bailey said coming up behind her. "You look like you're headed to the pool. It's not a water aerobics day is it?"

Sugar turned and flashed Dick a smile. "No, Dick. I swim laps three days a week. It's good exercise. I've got to do something to keep my girlish figure in shape."

Dick smiled wide, his perfectly white, perfectly false teeth were just a tad too large and made him a little horsey looking, but he had nice eyes—they were still a clear blue despite his seventy-nine years.

"And it is a beautiful shape, indeed," he said using a velvet voice. He had been on the radio years ago. A DJ. She loved to listen to his stories at dinner.

"Why, thank you," she said coyly. "What about you, Dick, what are you going to do for exercise today?"

"I was gonna head over to the exercise room and maybe bowl a little." There was no bowling alley at Summerfield—just a sixty-inch television and that video game that allowed you to interact with what was going on the screen. A lot of folks liked to bowl, or play tennis, or even shoot arrows. It made it much easier using a controller than having to actually pick up a bowling ball, but it got the heart rate up and there was always a crowd, which made it fun.

"Well, you have a good time. I'll see you at lunch."

"You certainly will," Dick said, giving her a wink and heading in the opposite direction, toward the exercise room. A few minutes later, after claiming one of the chairs around the outdoor pool, Sugar slathered on some sunscreen and dove into the clear aqua-colored water. She fell into her rhythm easily, counting the laps in her head. She swam vigorously using a freestyle stroke.

Head down, head to the side—breathe.

Her thoughts went to the conversation she'd had with her daughter the night before. Susan wanted her to talk to these women who were supposed to get rid of the ghosts in her brother's house. "No one can do that, except maybe a preacher, Susan," she'd said. Why did this always come back around to haunt her?

You know why, she'd heard her sister's distant voice say. She had made some excuse about having to go because one of her shows was about to come on, and she couldn't miss it. She hated putting Susan off, but Sugar just did not have the wherewithal to deal with the subject, and NCIS was coming on, so it wasn't really a lie. She just loved that Mark Harmon. So handsome.

Cold fingers dragged over the skin of her legs and she kicked harder. She must have hit an icy patch. She would have to remember to tell one of the girls in the exercise center. The pool was supposed to be heated during the off-season. Late-April brought very warm days, but the water wouldn't have been sufficiently warmed without the solar heater.

Ignoring the cold, she kept going until she hit the end of the pool and turned, heading toward the other end. Cold fingers wrapped around one of her ankles, chilling her to the bone. It dragged her under for a moment and her arms flailed. She kicked with her free foot. The air in her lungs grew stale, and if she didn't get to the surface soon, they would begin to burn.

Whatever was holding her down let her go, and she broke through the surface of the water, gasping in air and water, coughing until her chest ached. She turned 360 degrees, scanning the water below her. What had grabbed her? The sun sparkled off the top of the clear water, making wavy yellow-white lines on the blue pool bottom. There was nothing there. She was alone in the pool. It was too early for the lifeguard and she was really the only one who liked to swim this early in the year. Maybe she'd just imagined it.

Of course, you did. You silly, stupid old woman. You just spooked yourself with thoughts of the old house. She laughed, and it echoed across the water. She started her lap again —there were still five more to do. Within two laps, the rhythm put her at ease.

Head down, head to the side—breathe.

The sound of splashing water from her feet and arms working in harmony gave her a sense of satisfaction. She was lucky. She still had her health. So many here didn't. As long as she could stand up on her own, she was going to do whatever it took to keep this old body working. Nearing the last lap, she looked forward to getting out of the pool and sitting in the sun. Her muscles always felt so good after. Tired. Worked. Useful. If there was anything she wanted, it was to be useful.

Then why aren't you helping me? her sister's distant voice asked.

Sugar kicked off from the poolside, ignoring the voice. It'd been a long time since she'd heard it, and she had done everything in her power to avoid it—including staying away from her parent's home. It had broken her mama's heart, and maybe it meant she was hard-hearted —but really, she just couldn't face Honey again.

Icy fingers dragged across her back, down her leg, sending a chill through her again and she stopped mid-stroke. Her heart beat hard in her throat and she twisted around in the pool.

"Stop it, Honey," she said in a harsh whisper. "You go on now. Leave me alone."

Hands wrapped around both ankles this time, yanking her to the bottom of the five-foot-deep pool. They held her underneath, and she struggled, kicking as best she could at her invisible captor. Air bubbles rose around her and the burning in her lungs came fast, like a brush fire out of control. Grayness invaded the edges of her vision. An icy finger brushed across her cheek, forcing her to look up. Honey Talmadge floated in front of her eyes. Her dirt-streaked face and stringy hair looked exactly as it had that night nearly seventy years ago. The night she had died.

Sugar—please. Please?

Sugar felt herself rising, yanked at the waist, dragged over the coping. She was vaguely aware of shouting. Someone pushed her onto her side and raised her arms above her head.

"Mrs. Blackburn? Come on, Mrs. Blackburn—you gotta spit it out."

A hard knock on the back—once, twice. Sugar coughed and water spilled over her lips.

"That's it, Mrs. Blackburn. You breathe. Just keep breathing."

Sugar opened her eyes. One of the water aerobics instructors—she couldn't remember her name, Tiffany? Tiani? she just couldn't remember names very well anymore—smiled down at her.

"I'm still breathing," Sugar rasped. She pushed herself up to sitting and scanned the water. Sunlight glittered across the top. She coughed.

"What happened?"

"Leg cramp," Sugar lied with a smile. "The water's a bit colder than I expected."

"You know you really shouldn't be out here by yourself. It's always better to swim with a buddy." Tiffany (or was it Tiani?) scolded and wrapped a towel around the old woman's shoulders.

Sugar patted the young woman's hand. "You're right, dear. I'll remember that next time."

CHAPTER 12

When Susan had called and asked her to dinner on Tuesday, Charlie agreed, but only if they didn't have to meet at the house. She wasn't quite ready to face Aldus Talmadge again, especially not on his turf. Charlie had suggested Maudie's Seafood in Palmetto Point. The back of the restaurant overlooked the Stono River, and wasn't too far for either of them. The view at sunset was always spectacular on a clear evening and the food was so good it attracted locals and tourists. Charlie arrived first and asked to be seated outside on the breezy deck. She might as well enjoy herself while she was here. Perusing the menu, she waited for Susan to arrive.

Some part of her hoped that Susan's son Jason would be with her, even though she found him obnoxious. The dream about the girl in the convenience store kept gnawing at her. He'd said something about taking missing person reports. Maybe he would be able to tell her if the girl from her dream was really missing or not. If she wasn't, maybe she could somehow convince him the girl needed help. Despite their little run-in at the library, she sensed he took his job seriously. If a girl were in trouble, surely, he'd have to listen to her, wouldn't he?

"Hi," Susan said in a chipper voice as she approached the table. "Thank you so much for meeting me." She carried a tote bag with her and Charlie could see two large, old-fashioned scrapbooks poking out.

"Hi, Susan—what do you have there?"

"Well, you told me you were looking for some history on the house and I remembered that my mother had received a couple of packages my uncle had sent before he died. So, I went to her storage facility and dug these out. I'm hoping that maybe there'll be some information in there for you."

"Thanks." Charlie pulled the first book out of the tote bag. It was large and leather-bound. She opened it to the first page. The spicy scent of old paper wafted up, tickling her nose. There were clippings and envelopes stuffed inside the pages along with photographs—some of them very old, and very fragile—attached to the black paper with little triangular photo mounts that had turned yellow with age. Her fingers skimmed across the names and addresses on the top letter and images flashed before her eyes. Distant voices filled her head. Her breath caught in her throat for a moment as she realized there was still a lot of powerful energy attached to the letters.

May 15, 1890

My dearest Willet,

I have nowhere to send this letter, as it will be many months before you return from your journey at sea. My dear husband, I am at my wits end with our youngest son. His behavior has been more than deplorable, especially in the way he prances about trying to impress the colored girls tending the fields. It is difficult to write such things, and I have spent much time praying upon it. All I can do is hope for your quick return, as I can no longer control him or his lustful proclivities. I have taken to locking him in his room. Threats do not work and I do not have the stomach or heart to take a cane to him. He refuses to go to church and will not receive Reverend Higgins. I fear for his very soul, and for the reputation which is the foundation of our family name.

I will continue to pray for strength and wisdom. Please return to me soon.

All my love, Eleanor

.   .   .

CHARLIE PICKED HER HAND UP, NO LONGER WANTING TO feel this woman's disgust and pain. Her hand drifted to her mouth.

"Charlie?" Susan asked. "Are you all right?"

Charlie swallowed hard and forced a smile. "Yes, I'm fine," she said. "Sometimes, when I touch old things I pick up on leftover energy, I guess."

Susan's eyes widened, and she leaned forward, a glint of fascination sparkling in her eyes. "Really? What sort of energy?"

"Sometimes, I see or hear things. This letter," she said, pointing to it, not wanting to touch it again, "is from one of your ancestors. Eleanor Talmadge. She was writing her husband Willet about their youngest son and his bad behavior. I think, though I can't be certain that she was talking about Aldus Talmadge."

"Oh, my gosh," Susan said. "Well, we all know about Aldus Talmadge, don't we?"

"Yes. I suppose we do." Charlie traced her fingers around the edge of her water goblet. "You know, I've dreamed about him."

"You have?"

"Yes. He attacked a young black woman and ultimately killed her, I think by burying her alive."

"Oh, my lord." Susan sat back, astonishment lining her thin face.

"Do you mind if I borrow these and go through them later? I promise, I'll take good care of them."

"No, course not, that's why I brought them."

"I have two other things I wanted to ask you."

"Sure." Susan leaned forward. "Anything."

"Do you think your mother would be interested in talking to me?"

Susan grew quiet and her gaze shifted to the menu laying in front of her. "I tried talking to her about it, and she put me off. She's real funny about that old house."

"Why is that?" Charlie asked. "You mentioned she left and never went back. That must've been hard on your grandmother."

"Oh, I don't know about that," Susan said. "My grandma was made of stee,l but I guess you'd have to be if you'd been through what she had."

"What do you mean?"

"Oh you know, living through the depression. They lived in a big house but they were dirt poor and she lost at least two children before they turned five, and then of course there was my aunt's murder."

"Your aunt? Your aunt was murdered?"

"Yes. It happened when my mother was only twelve or thirteen, I think. A man took my aunt, she was sixteen or seventeen. Anyway, he raped her and killed her. From what I understand, my mother witnessed part of it."

"Oh, my God. No wonder she doesn't want to go

back," Charlie muttered under her breath. "Do you know what happened?"

"Not specifically. My mother won't talk about it. The only reason I even know about it is because sometimes my grandma would come and stay with us. See, after my mama and daddy married, they moved to Charlotte, which is where I grew up. So, one time, my grandma was visiting, I must have been about twelve, anyway, she was terrified for me to go anywhere alone. You have to remember, this was years before the notion of stranger danger. I asked my mother why my grandma was so afraid and she told me it was because of my aunt and what had happened to her. Although, even then Mama's recollection of it was still vague. Probably to protect me. I didn't know exactly what had happened until I started looking through some of the scrapbooks. There are several articles about it. In fact, there are several articles from before then, about young women who disappeared from the island. Why my grandma or Uncle Butch collected that stuff, I have no idea, but they did. Hopefully, you'll find it useful."

Charlie nodded. "Absolutely. This is exactly the kind of thing I need to arm myself with. So, I know exactly what I'm up against."

"Can I ask you a question?" Susan lowered her voice and glanced at the other tables around them, as if she was making sure no one was listening.

"Sure," Charlie said.

"What happens, exactly? You know, when you...see a ghost?" Susan whispered the last few words.

Charlie picked up her water goblet and took a sip. "I don't always see them. Sometimes, I hear them. Sometimes, I feel them, and sometimes I dream about them."

"I would be scared to death if I saw a ghost," Susan said.

"Sometimes, it can be scary, and sometimes I don't even realize they're dead right away."

"How can you not realize they're dead?"

Charlie shrugged. "Not all spirits are ghostly apparitions. Sometimes, they appear to be as solid as you and me. I've had whole conversations with people who seemed very much alive and it wasn't till after that it dawned on me—oh, hey, that guy was dead."

Charlie laughed and Susan joined her.

"Then there are times they make me work for it."

"Work for it, how?" Susan said, intrigued.

"Well, for instance, Aldus Talmadge is making me work for it." Charlie paused, straightening her silverware.

"He is?"

"Yeah. I didn't exactly see him when I went to your house. At one point, you touched me, and I sensed a man in my head—arrogant, shrouded in darkness. He didn't want to show me his face. I thought maybe he had attached himself to you, but I was wrong about that."

"Why were you wrong?"

"Because I dreamed about him last night, and then after I woke up, I saw him in my kitchen."

"Oh, my God. I would have died on the spot." Susan's voice rose to a shrill pitch and Charlie noticed a lady at a nearby table staring at them. "How long have you—you know—seen ghosts?"

"Since I was about five. I had an older sister, and when she was eight, she died of meningitis."

"Oh, sweetie, I'm so sorry for your loss."

"Thank you, I appreciate that. I didn't even know that she had passed at the time. I just woke up, and she was standing at the end of my bed and she looked normal to me. I couldn't understand what she was doing at home because she had been taken to the hospital the day before. She said she just wanted to play with me, which I remember thinking was weird because she never wanted to play with me...but I also didn't care. So, at two o'clock in the morning, we played with my tea set and my dolls. And I remember giggling with her because we were getting away with something being up that late and then she told me I should get back to bed and she laid down next to me, and when I woke up in the morning, she was gone and my parents were in the kitchen crying. I tried to tell my father about her visit and he got so angry at me. I cried so hard because he thought I was lying to him. That I was making it up. Luckily my grandmother lived with us, and she came to me later and asked me about it. She was—well, she was like me. She hugged me and told me it was okay not to talk to daddy about it because it would just upset him. That was my first lesson in hiding my ability."

Susan's eye's popped wide open. "Oh, wow. That is amazing and sad. I guess it's lucky though that you grew up with a grandmother that at least knew—"

"Yeah—" Charlie forced a smile. There was no point in sharing the rest of her sob story. Charlie tipped her head and looked over Susan's shoulder. "Can you tell me something?"

"I can try," Susan said, glancing down at the menu in front of her.

"Is there a reason Jason doesn't like me?"

"Oh, sweetie, please don't take that personally. That has more to do with me than with you, I'm afraid. I've been going to psychics since Jason's father left me, and he absolutely hates it. He thinks all psychics are charlatans just out to make a buck and I'll admit I've met a few who weren't exactly scrupulous. But I've also encountered the real deal on occasion. You, my dear, are the real deal."

Charlie leaned in. "How do you know?"

"You know, for the longest time in my life, I didn't trust my own intuition. Which just means I've made a lot of mistakes in my life, including marrying Jason's father," Susan said. "A while ago now, I took a couple of self-improvement courses in learning how to listen to my intuition and ever since I started trusting it, I've been better off. My intuition tells me I can trust you, Charlie."

"Well, thank you. I really appreciate that, and I'm gonna do everything I can to help you."

"I know you will." Susan gave her a wink. "My intuition tells me so."

CHAPTER 13

"Yes, ma'am," Jason Tate said. "I fully understand. How long has she been missing?"

The woman's hands shook as she reached into her bulky purse and pulled out a framed picture of her niece Daniela Gutierrez. "Since Friday night."

Jason took the picture, opened the frame, and pulled out the girl's image. The girl looked closer to twenty than fourteen. Her large brown eyes drew him in. *Where are you?*

"And you're just now reporting it?" He tried not to sound too judgmental, but sometimes it was hard.

"I was told on Saturday that I had to wait. And I had to work yesterday so I couldn't come." The woman sounded defensive.

"All right." Jason nodded, trying to keep his voice neutral. "So, you're her guardian?"

"Yes. Her parents were killed in a car accident when Daniela was very small."

"And she was supposed to be where?"

"She was supposed to be with her friend Soledad."

"But she wasn't."

The woman sat back in the heavy wooden chair and hugged her large purse to her chest. "No." She spoke softly. "She—she snuck out to meet a boy. And Soledad said she never returned. She was supposed to be back by one a,m. That was their agreement."

"All right. That's some place to start. Do you know what boy?"

The woman's lips quivered, and she shook her head. "Not exactly. Soledad could only give me a first name."

"So he wasn't a boy Soledad knew? Maybe from school?"

Ms. Gutierrez's eyes welled and big fat tears spilled onto her round cheeks. She sniffled. "Soledad said she met the boy online. Said he was older."

The pit of Jason's stomach wrenched, and he pursed his lips, focusing on the notepad in front of him. A boy with no last name from the internet. Great. He was probably some fifty-year-old predator who got his rocks off on little girls. This was his fourth case of girls almost identical to Daniela—all under eighteen, meeting some guy they met on the internet, never to be heard from again. He tried to remain objective, but sometimes it just made him hate humanity. He understood why his partner Dale went home and downed a six-pack every night.

"All right, I need Soledad's information then—address and phone number if you have it."

"Of course." Ms. Gutierrez reached inside her large purse and pulled out her cell phone. She thumbed through her contacts before finally handing the phone to him. "This is Soledad's cell phone number."

"What about Daniela's computer? Any chance I could take a look at that?" Jason asked.

Ms. Gutierrez pulled a laptop from her bag and handed it to him. "I don't know the password."

"Don't worry about that. We've got technicians that can handle that." Jason put the laptop on his desk next to her photo.

Ms. Gutierrez glanced at the clock on the wall. "Do you need more information? I have to be at work in an hour."

"No, I think we have everything we need." He gave her his best reassuring smile and took one of his business cards from the holder on his desk. He handed it to her. "If you think of anything else, please don't hesitate to call me."

The woman stared down at Jason's card for a moment,

clutching it until the thick stock crinkled. "Do you think you will find her?"

"I'm gonna do my best."

"Thank you, Lieutenant." She smiled sadly and rose from the seat. He watched as she made her way across the office and disappeared into the hallway. He spent the next few minutes making a folder for Daniela Gutierrez and when he was done, he threw it on top of the other four cases. In his gut, he knew they were all related and that none of these girls had come to a good end, but until there were bodies to go with their faces, they were just more girls on a stack of all the other missing kids and runaways.

"Hey, Tate," Marshall Beck said, approaching his desk. "I got that information you wanted."

Jason's ears perked up, and he held out his hand. "Yeah? Let me see."

Marshall stopped just short of his desk and cocked his fat head. Marshall had let himself go since his wife left him. Not that he was Mister Universe before, but now his puffy face and balding head made him look more like a fat Mister Clean.

"I don't remember there being a case open on this chick." Marshall held the folder open against his man boobs.

"She's a person of interest in a case," Jason said

standing up and grabbing the folder from Marshall's grubby hands.

"Yeah, sure," Marshall said. "You think I didn't get a look at her? She's a hottie even in her driver's license photo, and that's saying a lot. You sure you're not just trying to weed out some psycho girl you want to date?"

"You are one sick bastard, you know that?" Jason said. "Trust me, this girl is up to no good, and I'm gonna make sure she doesn't hurt anybody."

"Crazy maybe, but up to no good? I'm not so sure. Looks like she's more likely to hurt herself, than anybody else," Marshall said.

"Why? What'd you find?" Jason scanned the folder and stared down at the photocopy of Charlotte Grace Payne driver's license attached to a copy of an admittance form. There was a hint of a smile on her lips and Marshall was right. On first glance, she was definitely hot. But it didn't matter how good-looking she was if she took advantage of older women scared out of their minds. He scanned through the document. Bingo. There it was. "How'd you get this?"

Marshall smiled. "Finesse. Maybe you should learn how to use it sometime."

"Yeah. You'll be the first one I come to for that." Jason smirked. No wonder she hated psychiatrists so much. Charlie Payne was certifiably crazy. Crazy enough to be admitted to the psyche ward at MUSC hospital, anyway.

CHAPTER 14

C harlie clutched her purse straps tightly against her shoulder as she followed the officer to Jason Tate's desk. Dread coiled tightly in her belly. She couldn't stop thinking about the girl from her dream. Jason Tate may not have been a fan of hers but she felt more comfortable talking to him about what she'd seen in her dream than a random officer. Getting him to take her seriously, that would be the challenge. She saw him sitting at his desk typing something into a computer and she stopped in her tracks and almost turned back. Jason looked up, his gaze zeroing in on her.

Too late now, Charlie. She forced a smile, and he scowled in return. *Great. This ought to be fun.*

"Tate," Deputy Marshall Beck said, a smug grin on his face. "You've got a visitor."

"I sure do," Jason said, pushing to his feet. "Well if it isn't Charlie Payne. To what do I owe this honor?"

Charlie stepped forward, her gaze flitting between Jason and the other deputy. "I need to talk to you about something. Privately, if possible."

Jason and the other deputy exchanged a look but Jason finally nodded and led her to an open interrogation room.

"Have a seat." Jason pointed to the chair facing the mirror on the wall. She watched enough television to know that the mirror was probably two-way and there were also little cameras mounted in the corner, their lenses pointed directly at the table. The chair made a scraping noise across the linoleum floor when she pulled it out and took a seat.

"What is this all about, Ms. Payne?" He sounded irritated already. Maybe this had been a bad idea. Maybe she should've just called in the tip anonymously.

"There's no real easy way to say this without you rolling your eyes at me but I have to tell somebody."

Jason took the seat across from her. He leaned forward. "All right, I'm listening."

"There is a girl. Maybe fourteen or fifteen. I think she's gone missing and I think I know who did it."

"All right," Jason said. His intense eyes narrowed. "Do you have a name?"

Charlie swallowed. "The girl or the man?"

"Either would be good," Jason said.

"No," she answered softly. "I only know what they look like and that he's an employee at a convenience store."

"Okay—what's the name of the store?"

"Well, I—" She shifted in the cold metal seat. "I don't know that either."

Jason leaned back in his chair. He scrubbed his hand over his mouth and chin as if he were unsure what to say. After a moment, he blew out an irritated sigh. "So, there's a girl whose name you don't know who may have been taken by some man whose name you don't know. But you know he works at a convenience store but you don't know that name either." His irritation edged toward anger. "How exactly did you get this information?"

Charlie licked her lips and avoided his unforgiving glare. "I dreamed about it."

Jason's eyebrows raised halfway up his forehead and his jaw tightened. "You dreamed about it?"

When she was younger, she would have shrunk away from the scorn in his voice. But when she left Scott, she'd sworn to herself that no one would be allowed to make her feel so small again. She straightened in the uncomfortable chair and met his gaze. "Yes."

Jason rolled his eyes and shook his head. "You are wasting my time." He started to rise from his chair.

"No, wait, please." She grabbed his hand without thinking, and touching him sent a shock up her arm. She dropped his hand and took a step back, instinctively rubbing her palm with the thumb of her other hand. A black mist formed behind Jason. It grew darker, and the form became more human until finally the apparition of a man appeared. He looked like an older version of Jason with gray at his temples, only his eyes were bright blue instead of hazel. His legs were more mist than man and he hovered next to Jason. The man must have been Jason's father and Charlie couldn't take her eyes off him.

"You knucklehead, what is wrong with you?" the man asked. "Is that the way you treat a beautiful woman? Did I not teach you anything?"

The snap of Jason's fingers in front of her face diverted her attention.

"What is wrong with you?" Jason asked.

Charlie chuckled to herself. It looked like Jason was more like his father than his mother, even echoing the same words.

"Nothing," she said. "Is your father alive?"

"No, I am not." The older man looked at her. "You can see me, can't you?" He clapped his hands together and strangely it made a noise that made Jason glance over his shoulder in his father's direction.

"Hallelujah," Jason's father said. "Finally—I need you to tell my knucklehead of a son something for me, so I can get out of here."

"How is that any of your business?" Jason asked.

"Do not listen to him. It is plenty your business if you can see me," the older man said.

"You're right, it's not my business. I just—when I touched you—" Her eyes flashed toward the older Tate.

"You know I can arrest you for touching me," Jason threatened.

The older Tate shook his head. "Will you tell my son he's an idiot?"

"No," Charlie said glancing at the apparition. "That's mean. I'm not gonna tell him that."

"You're not gonna tell who, what?" Jason put his hands on his hips. She knew the look on his face. Scott had given her the look a thousand times during their marriage—the Charlie's-crazy-look.

Charlie frowned. Well maybe she would after all. "I'm not going to tell you that you're an idiot. No matter what your father wants."

"What the hell are you talking about?"

"Your father and those are his words, not mine, by the way."

"My father?"

"I see what you did there." Jason's father waggled a finger at her and grinned. "You're a spunky thing aren't

127

cha?" Jason's father looked her up and down. "A little on the skinny side, but still, I like you."

"Yes. Your father is here," Charlie said softly.

"That's not funny." Jason's usual irritation with her dissipated.

"Good, 'cause I'm not joking." Charlie refused to back down. Maybe this was the only way she would get him to believe her. "So when did your father pass away?"

"Hello! I'm still here. Obviously, I haven't passed anywhere. Sheesh." The older Tate folded his arms across his see-through chest. Charlie noticed the clothes the apparition wore were stained with both sweat and blood.

"What happened?" Charlie shifted her attention to the spirit.

"Why don't you tell me? You're supposed to be the psychic," Jason scoffed.

"He doesn't believe I can talk to you," Charlie said.

"Yeah, he always was thick. Just like his mother."

Charlie scowled. "You know you keep making cracks like that, and I won't help you."

Jason's eyes widened, and he took a step back. He glanced at the closed doo,r as if he was trying to determine the best way to get out of her presence.

"I'm sorry. I'm sorry. I'll be good. I promise." The older Tate held up his hands in surrender.

Charlie shrugged. "Fine. What is it you want him to know?"

The apparition turned to his son and looked him up and down. He sighed, even though he couldn't really breathe anymore and scrubbed his chin with his hand. Charlie had seen this a lot with spirits. So many times their mannerisms followed them into death.

"All right, tell him that in that box I left him, there is a key. He wanted to know what it was for. It's to a bus locker at the Atlanta bus depot. He knows the one I'm talking about. Tell him I left him something in that locker."

"I don't know what your problem is, Ms. Payne, but I think this conversation is over." Jason reached for the door. "Thank you for the tips. And I'll look into it."

"You father wants you to know the key you found in the box he left you is to a bus locker in the Atlanta terminal. He says you know the one I'm talking about. He wants you to know there's something that he left you in that locker."

Jason's face blanched. "Oh, yeah? Anything else?"

Charlie glanced toward the older Tate.

"Yeah," Mr. Tate said. "Ask him what the hell was he thinking wasting a whole bottle of Johnny Walker?"

Charlie struggled to look at Jason for a minute. It was always the really personal things that she hated conveying when they were unwanted. It almost never made a believer out of those who refused to see the truth. Lisa had once told her it was cognitive dissonance. Sometimes people just couldn't get past long-held beliefs, no matter what their ears and eyes told them.

"What, you're not gonna tell him?" the older Tate asked. He threw his hands up in the air. "What the hell good are you?"

"Just so you know, your father's a jerk," Charlie said turning away from the apparition.

"Oh-kaaay," Jason said, drawing out the word.

"Just my luck," Jason's father ranted. "I finally find someone who can hear me and she hates me."

Charlie blew out a heavy sigh and glared at the spirit. Passing on his message looked to be the only way to get him to shut up. "Fine," she said. "Your father wants to know why you would waste a whole bottle of Johnny Walker like that?"

Jason's eyebrows shot up and he opened the door to the interrogation room, ushering her out. "Yeah it's time for you to go now."

"Wait. Please tell me that you'll consider what I told you about. And if it helps, the convenience store had a logo on the gas pumps. It was a hare and turtle."

"Yeah, I'll keep that in mind. Thanks," Jason said curtly. He nudged her elbow. "Bye-bye now."

Charlie turned and walked away. She could feel Jason staring a hole through the back of her head. She was glad when she stepped into the elevator and the doors closed behind her, freeing her from the weight of his glare.

CHAPTER 15

Jason sat in the waiting room of the West Ashley offices of Low Country Women's Care, thinking about his encounter with Charlie Payne. He had almost convinced himself that his mother might have said something to her about the key in the box—but his mother only knew about the box, not its contents. And how the hell did she know about the whiskey he'd poured on his father's grave? He had never told anyone about that, not even his mother. He wanted to believe Charlie was a fraud, a con artist, but those things she knew were personal. Too personal.

Three pregnant women were in the waiting room with him. One leafed through an old copy of *Southern Living* and the other two eyed him suspiciously, keeping their hands protectively over their bellies. The woman with dark curly hair sitting across from him kept glancing from his face to his gun. He gave her a smile, but she clutched her belly tighter.

"Officer Tate." A pretty young nurse appeared at the door leading to the back offices. "Dr. Carver will see you now."

Jason gave the woman across from him a nod and rose to his feet. He followed the nurse through the maze of hallways to Scott Carver's office. A heavy cherry desk was centered in the large space in front of a floor to ceiling window overlooking the marsh behind the building. Carved cherry bookshelves full of medical books lined the far wall and two leather chairs faced the desk.

"You can wait in here. He'll just be a few minutes," the nurse said. She closed the door behind her and he walked around looking at the titles of the books and the collectibles displayed among them. There was a baseball signed by Babe Ruth inside a clear acrylic case. A framed Atlanta Braves Jersey hung on the wall and an array of pictures in black frames with white mats hung inside the bookshelf. Each one had a label and was of the doctor and what Jason presumed was his son. Fishing at Edisto Beach. Sailing in the Caribbean. Fly-fishing in Montana. Surfing in Hawaii. Paddle boarding at Folly Beach. Kayaking down the Edisto River. They looked happy in every photo. They also looked like they belonged inside an outdoorsman's catalog. Of course there were no pictures of Charlie, but why would there be?

The door opened and Dr. Scott Carver walked through with his hand extended. He smiled and his perfect, white teeth gleamed. Jason could see why they had been together. She was gorgeous, and he looked like he belonged inside the pages of a men's magazine. Jason wondered what exactly had torn them apart. Most men, in his experience, were willing to put up with a little crazy, especially with a wife who looked like Charlie Payne. Maybe she had become too much to handle or maybe she just didn't fit into the image the man had of himself.

"Hi," he said. "I'm Dr. Carver. It's Sergeant Tate, right?"

Jason took his hand and shook it. "Yes."

"Please take a seat." Scott pointed to the chairs and moved behind his desk to the high-backed leather chair. "So, how can I help you today?"

"As I said on the phone, I wanted to ask you a few questions about your ex-wife." The leather of the seat creaked as Jason sat down. He pulled a notepad and pen from his pocket.

"Charlie." Scott folded his hands and his expression became unreadable. "Is she in trouble?"

"I can't really comment on the case I'm working, but

she's come to me with some information, and I'm just following up."

"Information? What sort of information?"

"Sorry, I can't really go into an active investigation." It wasn't exactly a lie. He couldn't talk about an active investigation, but the good doctor didn't need to know the details of his real motives. "What I can say is that Ms. Payne has come forward with some information and there are some doubts about its validity."

"Really?" Scott said. "I'm not really sure how I can help you. Charlie and I really only see each other to facilitate our custody agreement."

Jason gave him a closed-mouth smile. "It appears there's been some allegations in the case I'm investigating. Your wife—"

"Ex-wife," Scott corrected.

"Right, ex-wife. Has come forward with some pretty extraordinary claims."

"Oh?"

"Yes, seems she thinks she knows something about a girl that's gone missing from one of the islands based on a dream."

Scott's jaw clenched. "Really?"

"Yes, and interestingly enough, some of the information seems to be true."

"I see." Scott's tone became curt. "I don't understand what this has to do with me."

"I'm just trying to get some background on her. It's my understanding she spent some time at MUSC for psychological issues."

Scott's face shifted into neutral, giving nothing away. "I see."

Jason smiled. "You see what?"

"Sergeant, I'm sure you've already checked her out, right? Seen her website?"

Jason stayed silent, keeping his gaze steady and Scott shifted in his chair again.

Scott scowled. "I'll take that as a yes." He fiddled with the small globe paperweight in front of him. "As you know, my ex-wife believes she's psychic."

"But you don't."

"There's no such thing. Don't get me wrong, I believe certain people can be highly intuitive. But trust me when I tell you this—there are no psychics. There are no dead people walking around needing someone like my wife—"

"Ex-wife," Jason corrected.

Scott's jaw clenched. "Ex-wife. There are no spirits waiting for Charlie to help them cross over to heaven or hell or wherever it is she believes they go."

"So, you're saying your ex-wife is a liar?"

"No—" Scott backpedaled and bitterness tinged his words. "Maybe. I don't know." Scott paused as if he were thinking about how to proceed next. His lips twisted into a grimace. "It's easy to get caught up in Charlie's web.

Don't buy into her delusions. It will lead you to places you don't want to go and honestly, it may jeopardize your case." Scott sat back in his high-backed leather chair and propped his chin up on his thumb and forefinger. "You know Charlie's had her problems."

Jason nodded. "What kind of problems?"

Scott hesitated. "Mental problems. If I were you, I would not take anything she says seriously."

"So, you were married, what? Eight years?"

"Yes."

"And in all that time, she never convinced you? Never connected you with a dead relative or—"

"No," Scott answered too quickly and sounded as if Jason had hit a nerve. The good doctor shifted in his seat and held his gaze too steadily on Jason's. One thing Jason knew about liars was they either couldn't look you in the eye, or they wouldn't look away while they lied. Scott Carver was lying. What Jason wasn't sure of, was if Scott was lying to himself. "She tried, but like I said, it's a delusion, and anything she may have come up with was just emotional blackmail."

"And I bet you told her, too, didn't you?" Jason leaned forward. "Is that why she tried to commit suicide?"

Scott tipped his chin up. "You know about that?"

"Like you said, I've checked her out."

"Then you know all you need to know about my wife. I really don't think there's anything else I can add."

"I see." Jason rose to his feet. "I think I've got everything I need. Thank you for your time. It's been very enlightening."

"Glad I could help."

Jason reached into the front breast pocket of his uniform, pulled out one of his cards, and left it on the desk. "If there's anything else you can tell me about Charlie, don't hesitate to call."

Scott glanced at the card as if he was afraid to touch it. "I will."

CHAPTER 16

"Is this it?" Lisa pointed to the screen of her laptop.

Charlie leaned in to take a better look. There it was. The turtle and hare logo she had seen in her dream. "Yeah, that's it," Charlie said.

"Hare's Swifty Mart and Gas," Lisa scoffed. "I guess this guy didn't really understand the tortoise and hare fable."

Charlie chuckled and wrote down the address. "I guess not. It's way out near the causeway leading to Talmadge Island."

"I don't think you should go out there. Especially not by yourself. You could just pass this info on to your little deputy friend, right? Let him check it out."

Charlie rolled her eyes. "Yeah, like he'd take me

seriously now. I'm going to have to gather some sort of evidence before he listens to me."

"So you don't think giving him the message from his father made him a believer?"

"No." Charlie shook her head. "Not by a long shot. I think it freaked him out, but it certainly didn't change his mind."

"Well you tried." Lisa shrugged. "I still don't want you going out there by yourself."

"Are you volunteering?"

"Maybe. What time are you thinking of going?"

"In my dream, it was night. And the digital clock read 11:39. I figure he must be a third-shift worker."

Lisa sighed and frowned. "Sorry, I've got a meeting at seven-thirty in the morning."

"Don't worry about it. I'll be fine. It's a public place, right?" Charlie's phone began to ring with Scott's ring tone. "Hang on. I have to take this."

"What the hell is going on with you?" Scott barked in her ear before she could even say hello.

"Well, good afternoon to you too," Charlie quipped.

"I just had a cop in my office asking me questions about you. Said you had gone to him with some crazy dream."

"Did he?" Charlie directed her gaze to Lisa. She held the phone away from her mouth. "Looks like Deputy dogged is being nosy again. Evidently he just questioned Scott about me."

"Who are you talking to?" Scott snapped.

"Lisa," Charlie said. "I'm sorry he bothered you, Scott. This really isn't about the information I gave him from my dream, though. He's just convinced that I'm going to take advantage of his mother."

"Abusing his power is more like it," Lisa grumbled under her breath.

"What did you tell him?" Charlie asked.

"He thinks you're unstable. He asked me if you could actually see ghosts."

"I bet you just loved that, didn't you?" Charlie chuckled. "What did you tell him?"

"I told him I don't know what you see. So you're not acting as some sort of psychic consultant?"

"No," Charlie said. "Like I said, he is hell-bent on proving I'm some sort of con artist."

"Oh." Scott grew quiet and his silence nagged at her.

"Scott—did he tell you I was a consultant?"

"He may have implied it. He had questions about you."

"What questions?" Charlie pinched the bridge of her nose. "What did you tell him?"

"He wanted to know if I believed in your special abilities." Scott sounded bitter. "He knew about your time at MUSC, by the way."

"Oh, my God, did you tell him why I was there?"

"No." Something in his tone said otherwise. Maybe he didn't say the words, but he didn't defend her, either, and she knew in her heart that he didn't take responsibility for his part. Anxiety snaked around her heart and gave it a squeeze.

"You know sometimes I really hate you."

"Charlie—" Scott started.

"I've got to go." She tapped End on the screen of her phone, not giving him a chance to finish his response. Icy dread dropped from her chest into her stomach. Now that Jason knew, she had no doubt he would dig in and try harder to discredit her. Crazy and Con-artist. No matter what he thought, she wouldn't let him stop her. There really was a missing girl out there and a malevolent spirit really was haunting his mother. She couldn't just turn away from those things.

"You okay?" Lisa placed a hand on Charlie's shoulder and gave a gentle squeeze.

"Yeah, I'm fine."

"So, sounds like Scott's still a jackass."

"Yeah, some things never change, I guess." Charlie's mouth curved into a weak smile. Thank God for Lisa and her levity.

Sugar leaned against the banister of the corner porch overlooking the golf course. She watched as a party of four men took turns hitting the little ball and shook her head. It might have been good exercise if they'd walked to the next hole, but they all climbed into a golf cart and drove off. She'd been afraid to go back into the pool since Monday. Thankfully, Honey had not made another appearance, at least not in person. Her dreams were another story. Honey seemed hell-bent on making her relive that long-ago night when she had run into the man who had killed her.

Susan had suggested that she talk to the young woman with the gift, but she wasn't sure what good would come from it. She took a sip of iced tea from the sweaty glass balancing precariously on the top of the banister.

Her cell phone rang inside her small apartment and she went to answer it. She frowned when she saw her daughter's picture and number on the phone. Susan had given her hell about buying the expensive piece of technology.

"What do you need with a smartphone?" Susan had nagged.

It came in handy for looking things up on the internet. She didn't drive anymore and sometimes she and a couple of her friends would book an Uber to take them shopping. She also liked using it for Facebook.

"Hello, Susan," Sugar said.

"Hey, Mama," Susan answered. "How are you doing today?"

"I'm doing very well, thank you. Is there something I can do for you?"

"I had lunch with the psychic lady the other day, the one I told you about, and she mentioned that she really would like to meet you."

"I already told you I don't need to talk to that woman."

"I understand Mama, but she needs to talk to you. I think she has questions that only you can answer. I've done my best, but some things I just don't know."

"I thought she was psychic. Shouldn't she know these things?"

"I don't think it works quite like that. So, will you meet with her please?"

"Oh, I don't know, Susan. I don't think there's anything I can tell her."

"I don't believe you, Mama."

"Excuse me?" Sugar said.

"I'm serious. Now if you won't call her, then I may just bring her over to see you. Do you want that?"

Sugar fiddled with the pad of paper she kept on the table with her cell phone charger. She considered her daughter's threat. Susan had become bold in her middle age. "All right. Fine."

"So, you're going to call her?"

Sugar sighed. She could have held out, but Susan could be so persistent and she just didn't want to deal with it. If giving in meant a little peace, then she'd take it. "Yes."

"Good, let me give you her number."

CHAPTER 17

J ason pulled into the parking lot of Hare's Swifty
Mart and Gas. It hadn't taken him long to find
the convenience store with a turtle and hare on
the logo. It was a tiny place with only four
pumps, but the location near the main road leading to
Talmadge Island made it a hot spot for teenagers. He
glanced at the stainless-steel diver's watch on his arm. It
was just after three p.m. and already a car full of teens
had parked along the edge of the parking lot to hang out.
He took the photo of Daniela from his pocket and
approached the car. Silence fell over the four teens—
three boys and a girl. One of the boys and the girl were
apparently a couple by the way their bodies tangled
together.

"Good afternoon," he said using his best

authoritarian voice. "I was wondering if any of you kids have seen this girl?"

They passed the photo around, each taking a good look. The girl looked shocked when it was her turn.

"This is Daniela," she said.

"You know her?" Jason asked.

"Sure, we go to school with her," the girl said.

"Have you seen her recently?"

The girl's dark eyes widened, and she shook her head. She handed the photo back to Jason. "No, sir."

"Do you know if she had a boyfriend?"

They all exchanged glances.

"You know she's missing, right?" Jason said. "Her aunt is going out of her mind with worry. If you know something, I'd really appreciate it if you tell me. I'm not trying to get her in trouble. I just want to make sure she's safe."

"Yeah, she's got a boyfriend," the boy sitting on the tailgate said. He pushed his baseball cap up farther on his head and frowned. "He's an older dude, though."

"College boy," one of the other boys said.

"Does college boy have a name?"

The boy with the cap shrugged. "I think she called him Tony, but that's all I know."

"All right," Jason said, reaching into his pocket. "Listen, if you hear from her or this Tony, I want you to give me a call, okay?" He handed each one of them a card.

"Like I said, I'm not trying to get her in trouble. I just want to bring her home."

They each gave him a solemn nod.

"Yes, sir," the girl said. "Do you think—?" she started but a look from one of her friends stopped her.

"What's your name?" Jason asked.

"Haley." The slim, pretty girl pushed her shoulder-length, brown hair behind one ear.

"You were gonna say something, Haley. I'd really appreciate it if you'd finish. Especially if it's a question or a concern you have."

"It's just—you know she's not the first girl who's just stopped coming to school."

"Yeah," Jason said. "I know. So, you know some of the other girls who've gone missing recently?"

"Just one, but I've heard about the others. It's kind of scary."

"Yeah," Jason said. "It is. That's why it's really important that you hang out with your friends and don't go off by yourself. And don't communicate with strangers online."

"You think this is about some dude she met online?" baseball cap boy said.

"That's what her aunt speculated. Do you know something different?"

"Me? Naw," the boy said. "I don't know anything about that. Just seems weird it's only been girls from the islands around here. Seems like an online stalker might have a wider range of opportunity."

"That's an interesting theory you have," Jason said. "I'll keep that in mind. Y'all be careful. You hear?"

"We will," the girl said. "I hope you find them."

Jason let his lips curl into a brief smile. "Me too. Call me, seriously, if you think of anything else."

Jason gave them a nod and headed inside to talk to the manager.

* * *

"Yeah, I've seen her here," the manager said. "But I can't tell you the last time. Maybe last week? Sorry."

"I have a source who says she was here last Friday night," Jason lied.

"Really? Well, I can always give you the surveillance for Friday night, if you want it. I just got these new cameras about a month ago. Totally high-def. Really crisp images." The manager shrugged. "We got robbed last year and the old video was pretty worthless."

"Yeah, that would be great," Jason said. "Can I have video for the weekend?"

"You betcha," the manager said. "Give me about ten minutes. I'll burn you a copy."

"Great," Jason said.

* * *

RAY KURTZ WALKED IN TO THE SWIFTY MART AND ZEROED in on the cop standing near the counter. He'd come in to get his paycheck so he could run it by the bank before they closed at five. There were two ways he could play this—he could be totally cool or he could just turn right around and come back later. He took a step backwards and started to pivot.

"Hey, Ray," Mikey, the day shift counter clerk called. "You want your check or what? Because if you don't want it, I'll take it."

"'Course I want my check." Ray stepped up next to the officer, not looking at him. Mikey opened the register and lifted the cash box out. He pulled a stack of four or five envelopes from beneath held together with a paper clip and thumbed through them until he found Ray's.

"Here you go," Mikey said. His eyebrow piercing glittered in the afternoon sun shining through the front window.

Ray snatched the envelope from Mikey's hand.

"So, you work here, too?" the cop asked.

Ray's jaw tightened, and he forced a smile.

"Yes, sir," he said. No need to raise any suspicions.

"Have you seen this girl?" The cop held out a photo of a young Latina girl. Her long dark curls cascaded over her shoulders and he was mesmerized by her bright white teeth, frozen in a smile forever.

"No, sir," Ray said, shaking his head. "Can't say as I have." His lips curved into a half-smile and he met the cop's gaze straight on. Where was the damn voice when he needed it? It was all for getting him in trouble, but was completely silent when faced with the possibility of the consequences from its yammering. Sweat dripped from the back of his hair in an itchy line down his back. The cop studied his face for a moment and he fought the urge to rub his hand across his neck. The cop's eyes narrowed.

"All right, deputy," the manager said, emerging from the back offices of the store. He handed the cop a shiny DVD in a paper sleeve. "Here ya go. Hope this helps you find the girl."

"Thanks," the cop said. He gave them all a nod and disappeared through the front door.

"What's wrong with you?" his manager asked. "You're as white as a sheet."

"Yeah," Ray said, fanning himself with the envelope in his hand. "I think I'm just a little overheated. Hot in here."

"Well, you better not call out sick," his manager said. "I don't have anybody else to cover the night shift."

"Don't worry, boss," Ray said. "I'll be here."

CHAPTER 18

Charlie pulled up to the first pump and filled her nearly empty tank. She scanned the parking lot, taking note of the video cameras on the exterior of the building. She removed her phone from her back pocket and glanced at the time. Her screen read 11:30 p.m. When the pump clicked off, she returned it to its cradle and reached inside her car for her wallet. Glancing up she noticed him standing at the glass door watching her. Her heart hammered in her throat. Aldus Talmadge. What was he doing here?

She had seen spirits attached to people and things, but she never encountered a spirit that could roam freely the way he did. Some part of her wished she could sit down with him and ask him questions, but she squashed that, letting her desire for him to just move on—preferably to hell—to take over.

She took a deep breath and headed in to pay for her gas.

Once inside the building, she pretended not to see him. It took real work not to flinch when he put his hand right in front of her nose.

She took a good look at the clerk behind the counter. He was not the man from her dream.

"Where's the candy aisle?" she asked.

The young man behind the counter looked up from his hot rod magazine and pointed to the aisle near the soda cooler. She took the long way around, winding her way past the bread, peanut butter, saltines, and cans of soup. She spotted a box of salt and picked it up.

There were four cameras that she could see—one in each corner. She wondered how many times this place had been robbed for the owner to make such an investment. This place was so far out she couldn't imagine it was that lucrative. But what did she know about running a convenience store? Maybe if she came back and spoke to the manager, she could somehow sweet-talk him into letting her look at recent footage? That was a stab in the dark, though. She wasn't even sure the girl had gone missing yet.

The doorbell sound rang out across the store and she looked up to see the man from her dream walk through the door. Aldus Talmadge had followed her around the store, but had stopped trying to speak to her when she ignored him. It surprised her that he didn't try to get her attention by throwing something at her, but maybe he was not quite that powerful. She had certainly encountered spirits who had learned to focus their energy on a particular task. In her experience, though, that ability was usually tied to great emotion. Fear. Anger. Even love.

Aldus disappeared from beside her and reappeared right behind the man from her dream.

"You're late, dude," the young man behind the counter said. He scowled.

"Not your problem, Dave," he said, slipping on an orange and green vest with a nametag attached to it.

Aldus whispered something in the man's ear and he stopped the argument with Dave before it really started. A feeling of déjà vu washed through her. Aldus leaned in close to the man and both the man and the apparition shifted their gazes toward her. An arrogant smile played at the corners of the spirit's lips.

Charlie refused to be intimidated. It had only been a dream. She had nothing to fear from the spirit, and as far as the man was concerned, she didn't think he would try anything with a coworker present, and all these cameras recording his every move.

She glanced down at the candy again and picked up a

bag of Skittles. They were Evan's favorite. She walked with her head held high, ignoring the staring man and glaring apparition.

"I got gas on pump two," she said, putting the salt and the candy on the counter. The man continued to stare at her, standing a little too close for comfort. She scowled and mustered her best imitation of Lisa. Staring him directly in the eyes she said, "Can I help you with something?"

He startled and his eyes widened. "No, ma'am," he said. His cheeks turned pink, and he looked away quickly.

"I'm gonna sweep the store," he announced.

"Fine," Dave said. "You do that."

The cash register dinged. "That will be $30.68."

Charlie opened her wallet, pulled out two $20 bills and handed them to Dave. After she left the store, she threw a glance over her shoulder before climbing into her car. The man stood at the window, holding his broom. His long, thin face was unreadable and Aldus Talmadge was nowhere in sight.

CHAPTER 19

"Duct tape, plastic ties, even handcuffs. I'm just saying, if it's out there, I can escape from it." Brian leaned back in his chair and put his hands behind his head. Charlie gave her coworker a bemused smile.

"Why would you even have to escape from those things?" Charlie asked.

"You know, in case I'm kidnapped," he answered, as if the question was stupid.

Charlie quirked an eyebrow.

"What? It could happen. People are crazy today. It's good to be prepared."

"Right," she muttered and shrugged. It wouldn't surprise her if Brian had a room in his house filled to the brim with freeze-dried rations, canned food, and weapons. Just in case there was a zombie apocalypse. She bit the inside of her lip to keep from showing her amusement. "So, how would you do it then?"

Brian pushed his glasses up on his nose, his round face lighting up. "Really?"

"Really."

"Okay. Just wait." Brian pulled his black backpack from the floor and began to dig through it. A moment later, he produced a half-used roll of duct tape.

Charlie folded her arms across her chest. "Do I even want to know why you have duct tape in your bag?"

"What? I always have some with me. You never know when you might have to fix something." His condescending tone was getting on her nerves. Hopefully, she would get a call soon. He shoved the thick gray tape at her until she took it. He pressed his wrists together and held them out. "Wrap me up."

"What?" Charlie scanned the call center floor for the closest supervisor. "No. You could get a call."

"Come on, it'll be fine." He pushed his hands closer toward her. "Bind me up."

Charlie sighed and ripped off a long piece of duct tape. She wrapped it tightly around his wrists.

"Great," he said. "Now, watch carefully. You may need to use this someday. You know, because women are kidnapped more than men."

"Sure." She raised her eyebrows and nodded. Brian

wasn't the craziest coworker she had, but he was a close second. Better to humor him than to argue.

"Now, watch carefully. I'm going to show you how to break these bindings." He raised his hands above his head.

Charlie's phone vibrated against her keyboard tray and she flipped it over and glanced down. At the top it read Evan. They talked almost every day, so it was rare for him to text and her first thought was that he was in trouble.

Mom? Can you call me?

Her heart skipped a beat.

"Charlie, you're not watching, seriously, how are you going to learn this?" Brian said. Charlie held up one finger, shushing him. She glanced at the application running in the corner of her computer screen that told her when her breaks and lunch were and how long she'd been in certain phone codes. Her second break wasn't for another forty-five minutes. She picked up the phone and quickly texted him.

I can on my next break. Can you wait till then?

"The illegal cell phone," Brian half-whispered. His papery-thin voice creeped her out as he said, "Is it your boyfriend?"

Charlie scowled at him. "My son, actually." She glanced around the call center floor looking for a supervisor, maybe Laura or Kaylee. They both tended to be more sympathetic when it came to child issues.

Two letters—*OK*—was his response. It was ridiculous to think that she could be so empathic as to feel his rejection and hurt through the text message, and yet that's exactly what she felt. It must've been important for him to text her at one-thirty on a Wednesday afternoon. Why wasn't he in class? And why was he texting her instead of his father? She laid the phone back down on her keyboard tray out of sight.

"Okay. Ready? Watch."

Charlie fought the urge to tell Brian where he could put his duct tape. She had more important things to worry about. But she'd worked with him a couple of years now and knew if she didn't just let him show her his trick, he would ask her about it until she finally gave in.

"Fine, go ahead." She sat back in her chair.

He raised his hands above his head again, pressed his hands together like he was praying. In a quick swing downward that reminded her of a weird karate chop, he struck his stomach with his hands and the duct tape snapped, tearing apart.

"See?" he beamed. "That's all there is to it."

"Great," she said. Kaylee passed by her row of cubicles and Charlie placed her headset on the desk and put her phone into an unavailable queue to avoid any further calls.

"You want to try it?" Brian asked.

"Yeah, maybe some other time." She turned away from him and called, "Kaylee!"

Kaylee wasn't much younger than she was. She had come to work at the call center when she was nineteen and had worked her way up to supervisor. Of all the supervisors, she was the most respected. Kaylee turned toward her name and Charlie waved.

"What's up?" Kaylee bent close so as not to distract the other call center reps.

"I need to take my break early. My son has an emergency." It wasn't exactly a lie. She was assuming it was an emergency because he never contacted her at work.

"All right," Kaylee said. She had two kids of her own, and maybe it was wrong for Charlie to play on that sympathy but she certainly knew Dylan would've made her wait and would've scolded her or worse for even looking at her phone.

"Thanks." She entered the correct break code into the phone, grabbed her purse and cell phone and walked out of the call center through the back door, avoiding Dylan. Quickly she accessed her son's number and clicked Call. It rang once, twice, three times.

"Mom?" His ten-year-old voice sounded stressed.

"Hey, baby," she said softly, heading outside the building for a little privacy. "What's going on?"

"I'm sorry to bother you at work."

"It's all right. I'm sorry I can't respond as quickly as I'd like. Is everything okay?"

"I don't know. I just wanted to talk to you."

"Okay—" Charlie said. "I'm all ears."

"You know how you told me that if I had any dreams that upset me I should tell you?"

"Yeah, of course."

"I had a dream."

"Okay. Well tell me what happened in the dream, so we can deal with it."

"I dreamed that Jackson Grosse and I were riding bikes and that he wouldn't wear his helmet. He said helmets were for babies. We were riding along and he hit a rock and ended up busting his head open on the pavement."

"Oh, sweetie," she whispered. "It was just a dream. Everybody has dreams. I'm sorry that it was so disturbing for you."

His voice began to shake. "Mom—it came true."

"What do you mean it came true?" she said cautiously.

"We were riding bikes today because it's a teacher work day and I tried to tell him."

"Tell him what?"

"I tried to warn him about wearing a helmet, but he

wouldn't listen. He just laughed at me, thought I was being a baby."

"Sweetie, where's Miss Cora?"

"She's downstairs in the kitchen. Mom, they had to take him away in an ambulance. There was blood." He choked. "Just so much blood."

"Okay, okay. Does daddy know?"

"No, I didn't call him. He doesn't like it when I talk about dreams like this."

"What do you mean, sweetie? Have you had other dreams like this?" The line grew very quiet. "Evan, I need you to answer me. Have you had dreams like this before? Dreams that have come true?"

His voice sounded so small when he responded that it made her heart ache. "Yes."

"And what did your dad say about them?"

"He told me they were just coincidences, and that no one can predict the future. Then he got mad, and said that maybe I was dreaming about things I wanted to happen." He choked back a sob. "Mom, I didn't want Jackson to get hurt. Really, I didn't. He's my best friend."

"Oh, sweetie, of course, you didn't." She wanted to cry right along with him. "It's okay. I'm gonna come and see you in a little bit. All right? And we're gonna talk about this some more. Now, I want you to listen to me very carefully—okay? You did not make this happen. What happened to Jackson was an accident. Not your fault. Your dreams are not some sort of—wish." She had to fight from spitting out the word. Damn Scott Carver. Damn him for making their son feel like this. She could not wait to get off work and give him a piece of her mind. "The things you dream may sometimes be scary, and they may even sometimes come true, and you know what? That is perfectly okay. You are perfectly okay just the way you are. Do you understand me?"

He sniffled. "Okay."

"I love you buddy," she said.

"Love you, too, Mom."

They hung up and Charlie gritted her teeth. Her break was almost up. Scott Carver was not going to do this to their son. He was not going to make him feel like a freak. The world would be happy to do that for him and she was determined to do everything in her power to make Evan strong enough to handle it.

SCOTT HAD GOTTEN THE HOUSE IN THE DIVORCE. IT probably could've been hers if she'd fought harder, but she couldn't have afforded to keep it even if she had. At least this way, Evan could stay in his room and his school district near his friends. She walked up the steps to the idyllic two-story house on Daniel Island and rang the bell. After a minute, she saw Cora, their housekeeper, through the sidelight. *Scott's housekeeper*, she reminded herself. She waved and gave a perfunctory smile.

"Oh, my goodness, I wasn't expecting to see you today, Ms. Carver," Cora said.

"I know. And it's Payne now. I dropped my married name when we—" Her voice trailed off.

"Oh, I'm sorry. I didn't realize," Cora said.

"Is Scott here?"

"Yes, ma'am, he is. Come on in. Just wait right here and I'll go get him." Cora relegated her to the foyer that opened to a beautiful double staircase.

It was a showpiece. Scott had insisted. He was from a family of old money where status still meant something. Of course, she had never cared about any of it. The amenities were nice, but they were never the point to her. All she ever cared about was how much she loved him. Scott, wearing a black apron, emerged through the formal living room—a room they barely ever touched when they were together. He had a red and white checked dishcloth slung over his shoulder. It struck her as an odd sight because Cora did all the cooking when they were married.

"Charlie?" He sounded surprised but not quite happy to see her. "What are you doing here? It's not your day."

"I'm quite aware of our schedule, Scott. I'm here because Evan called me. He was very upset."

"Yeah, I heard about Jackson. Thankfully, Evan's got

enough sense to wear his helmet. He called you about that?"

"Yes. He also called me to tell me that he had dreamed about it."

Scott had the face of what her grandmother would have called a well-bred gentleman. The first time Charlie met him she thought he belonged in some other era, where men of a certain status dressed for dinner, drank brandy afterward, and talked about taking over the world. She always teased that he must have been a British aristocrat in a past life because of his refined features and squared jaw that never hinted at a five o'clock shadow, and his ability keep his feelings hidden. Stiff upper lip and all that. There was only one exception, and it almost always involved her abilities to see ghosts and predict things.

"He told you about that, did he?" Scott narrowed his pale blue eyes and wiped his hands on the towel. He blew out a breath through his nose, making his nostrils flare. A bull about to charge. It was always the beginning of a blowout with him, and she couldn't seem to stop herself.

"Of course, he did. He knows that I'm not gonna think he's crazy or try to blame him when his dreams do come true."

Scott laughed awkwardly. "Now, just wait a minute. I've never told Evan he was crazy for having dreams."

"It doesn't matter what you said. That's how he's

interpreted it. He's also interpreted it as the dreams he has that come true are some sort of sick wish fulfillment. Nice parenting, Scott. Seriously. You should write a frickin' book on it."

"Hey—" His voice rose. "I never said that his dreams were wish fulfillment."

"You sure about that?" In her mind, she saw the scene unfold between father and son. The irritated, impatient tone. The words implying their son might be having bad thoughts about his friend. She took a deep breath and gritted her teeth. "Think very carefully about how you answer."

Scott's cheeks reddened. "You are not some freaking human lie detector—no matter what you believe." His fingers tightened on his hips. "And I would never tell him his bad dreams were some sick wish."

"You keep telling yourself that, Scott. Tell yourself whatever you think is going to get you through the day. But do not ever try to make our son feel like he is crazy. Because he is not."

"Well, he's also not psychic. No matter what you think."

"You would just hate that, wouldn't you? If he was more like me than you."

"Screw you, Charlie. I don't have to stand here and take this crap from you anymore."

"No, you don't. But you do have to deal with the fact

that Evan is upstairs right now feeling guilty for what happened to Jackson. He's blaming himself. And you know who I blame? You."

"Well, that's just ridiculous. What happened to Jackson was an accident."

"Yes, it was. Have you told him that?"

"I figured I would talk to him at dinner."

"Great. That's just frickin' great. You still don't get it, do you? Even after all these years. You are so thick sometimes. I swear to God—" She threw her hands into the air. "He adores you, you dumbass, and he takes everything you say to heart. It won't be that way forever. Why on earth would you push him away before he leaves on his own?"

Scott's eyebrows rose, and he looked as if she'd slapped him. "You think I'm pushing him away?"

"He's scared to tell you things. Scared of your judgment. Is that really the relationship you want to have with him?" She folded her arms across her chest and planted her feet. "And whether you like it or not, he may be like me. Which means dealing with it, instead of living in denial. I didn't fight you on custody or on alimony or anything. But if you try to stop me from being his parent, you will have the fight of your life, Scott Carver. Do you understand me?"

He narrowed his eyes, and she thought he might come at her with both barrels blazing, but his jaw unclenched and he gave her a look she hadn't seen in a long time. A look of acquiescence. "Damn you, Charlie."

"Right back 'atcha. Now, are we going upstairs or what?"

"I don't want to encourage this thing. Whatever it is," Scott said.

"He may outgrow it; a lot of people do. But you better realize he may not, and whether you encourage it or not, it may not go away. Don't alienate him because you don't believe in it. Loving him means loving all of him."

Scott's lips twisted into an angry grimace. If there was one thing she knew about her ex-husband, he hated losing. He gritted his teeth. "So, just what do you suggest we do?"

"We go upstairs and we talk to him. Remind him that we love and support him, and that none of this is his fault."

"What about the dreams? What am I supposed to do about the dreams?"

"You can start by not calling them crazy. If you don't want to deal with it, encourage him to call me when he has a bad dream."

"What? So, you can tell him he's psychic? And that it's gonna come true?"

"Just because he has a dream doesn't mean it's going to come true. It means he needs to be comforted, especially if it scares him or worries him. Whether his dreams come true or not, it is our job to make sure he understands he can't be afraid. He can't let it stop him from living."

"Won't that feel like a lie? I mean, it almost stopped you."

She would have preferred that he had just punched her. It would've been less painful. The tears stung the back of her throat faster than she could've anticipated and her face filled with heat at the same time her chest filled with the sharp sensation that only Scott seemed to be able to inflict.

"That's a low blow." She blinked fast, refusing to let the tears fall. "Even for you."

"Charlie, I didn't mean ..." he said, sounding confused.

"No. You never mean it, do you?" Swallowing the tears, she took a step backwards. "Come on, let's do this. I don't want to spend all night tearing each other apart. We got divorced specifically so we didn't have to do that anymore." She turned and headed up the steps not waiting for him to follow.

CHAPTER 20

Exhaustion crept into her shoulders, making her limbs feel like they were filled with wet sand. She pulled into the parking space outside of her townhouse and put her blue Honda Civic into park. Her fingers fumbled with the key in the lock of her door.

After the encounter in her kitchen the other night, she had poured a straight line of the fine salt in front of all the thresholds and windows to keep Aldus Talmadge out of her house and out of her dreams. She'd been extra careful, making sure to step over it when coming and going. With her mind on nothing but what had happened with Evan and a hot shower, she opened the door, and stepped inside. She dropped her keys on the table by the door and stopped. Her shoes ground against something under her feet and she cursed under her breath. She'd forgotten about the salt. She flipped on the foyer light and stared down at salt spread out across the laminate flooring. Her eyes scanned the downstairs floor as her brain caught up with what she was seeing.

Several clear footprints led into the kitchen. Blood roared in her ears, drowning out the sound of her breath. Her hand floated back toward the basket to grab her keys. She had hold of them when he stepped out of the kitchen and faced her. He wore a ski mask over his face. Within a second, she had her hand on the doorknob and turned it, but it wouldn't budge.

Pain seared across her scalp and she found herself yanked backwards and thrust forward against the steel door. Stars burst into her vision, and the coppery taste of blood coated her tongue. He grunted and wrapped one of his meaty hands around her neck. He lifted her up, and she kicked out, her shoe scraping against the dingy white paint, leaving one long black mark. Her vision grayed at the edges. She clawed at the hand restricting her breath. One nail ripped against the black leather gloves sending fresh pain into her senses.

Is that all that will be left of me? A black mark? No. No. No!

She stopped kicking and planted her feet, her thighs straining against the force of him dragging her backwards. She lifted one foot and brought it down as hard as she could on his foot, then shoved her elbow into his ribs. An *oofing* grunt escaped his mouth and his grip on her loosened. A desperate cry escaped her, and she lunged for the tall basket by the door holding a golf umbrella and a baseball bat that Scott had given her when she moved out. She had thought it ridiculous at the time, but took it without arguing. She wrapped her hands around the throat of the bat and struck out. A crack resounded through the short hallway as the heavy maple connected with his forearm and a guttural scream came from behind the mask covering his mouth.

Her doorbell rang wildly behind her, making her jump. A fist banged against the door. "Ms. Payne? Charlie? Charlie, I know you're in there. Charlie?"

She locked gazes with her attacker for one long second before he turned and ran out through the kitchen. She stumbled to the door and unlocked it. Jason Tate was the last person she expected to find on her stoop, but he was a welcome sight.

"Oh, my God, what happened?" He stepped into the apartment, slipping the bat out of her hands, leaning it against the wall.

Her whole body shook as she rushed through the words. "There's a man in my house."

His usual arrogance was gone, replaced by something she could only think of as cool-headed-cop-mode. He unsnapped the leather band holding his gun in place and slid the gleaming black piece from its holster.

"Stay here," he ordered.

"No," she whimpered. She could hate herself for it later, right now she didn't want to be left alone. "What if he comes back?"

"All right." His lips twisted into a half frown and he nodded. "Stay close to me."

She nodded and took the bat in her hands again, resting it against her shoulder. He stopped to glance down at the messy spray of salt on the floor. He flashed a questioning gaze at her.

"Salt." Her hands tightened around the throat of the bat. "I'll explain later."

The half-wall dividing the foyer from the living room gave them a clear view of the sparsely furnished space. A couch, a television, an old rocking chair with an afghan hanging over the back. The only pictures on the wall were of her son.

They made their way into the kitchen, where they found the back door swinging open in the breeze.

"Stay right here," he said. "I promise you, I'm just going to go around the building to check things out. Lock the door behind me, and then go into your living room and lock that door. I'll ring the bell when I come back."

"You promise to come back," she said.

"Absolutely." He touched her arm giving it a reassuring squeeze. "Don't open the door without using your peephole first. Understand?"

"Yes," she said, nodding.

She turned the deadbolt and watched him through the window as he disappeared into the darkness surrounding the long row of townhouses. She waited by the front door with her back against the wall, holding the bat firmly in her hand. A few minutes later, the doorbell rang and she let Jason in.

"There's no sign of him." He looked her over. "He got you good, didn't he? Your lip's bleeding and so is your forehead."

She touched her lip with her tongue and fresh blood filled her mouth.

"You didn't happen to get a look at his face, did you?"

"No, he had on a ski mask. All I could see were his eyes. He was wearing gloves too."

"Course he was." Jason sighed. "You know that goose egg on the front of your head at least warrants being checked out. Maybe I should run you over to the emergency room."

"No, please don't do that," she said. "My ex-husband's best friend is an ER doc and I don't want to run into him. If Scott hears about this, he won't let my son come visit me this weekend. Please?"

"Fine," Jason said, pressing his mouth into a flat line. "Do you at least have a first aid kit?"

"My ex is a doctor. I have the Ferrari of first aid kits."

"Come on, let's get you cleaned up."

* * *

CHARLIE'S HANDS SHOOK AS SHE PEELED THE PAPER FROM
the adhesive bandage. She had led Jason into the kitchen,
where she had splashed her face with cold water. She had
pressed a gauze pad against her lip to stop the bleeding.
The small gash in her forehead had been a more
persistent bleeder and Jason held a folded gauze pad
against the wound while she fumbled with the Band-Aid.

"Here, switch with me." Jason took the Band-Aid from
her. She pressed her finger against the thick wad of gauze,
applying pressure. She could still feel the warm, sticky
dampness seeping through.

"So, you don't have any idea who he could be?" he
asked, pressing the bandage to her forehead and taking
another from the box.

"No." She winced at the pressure. "My television and
computer were still here, so obviously he wasn't robbing
me."

"Well, we should look around, make sure nothing else
is missing. Jewelry. Firearms. Bags of salt." A grin played
at the corners of his mouth. She chuckled a little at his
attempt to lighten things up.

"If only it had worked," she quipped.

"What exactly does the salt do?"

"It keeps out unwanted spirits." She said it matter-of-
factly.

"Right," he muttered under his breath, but she caught the tone. Then he sat back and looked at his handiwork. "It's not pretty, but it'll do the job."

"Thank you." It struck her, not for the first time, that she liked his face, especially without the arrogant smirk he usually wore. The sharp angles were softened by his stubble and he had kind eyes. "You know, I don't know what would've happened if you hadn't shown up."

"You were hanging in there, from what I could tell." His lips curled into a half-grin.

"What I don't understand is why you're here. The last time I saw you, you had that look on your face."

"What look?"

"The Charlie's-crazy look."

Jason looked anywhere but at her and he chuckled deep in his throat. "Yeah, well. I'm sorry about that. Your —" He paused, seeming to consider his words. "Your message was a lot to take in."

"My message? You mean your father's message?"

He scrubbed his hand over his chin. "Yeah."

"So, you believe me now?"

Jason shifted in his seat, putting his hands on his knees. After a moment, he shook his head and met her gaze. "I don't know what to believe. I kept thinking about how you could know those things because nobody knew them but me. I thought maybe my mother had told you about the box I inherited from my father, and that you had guessed about the key. I even called my mother, and she swears she never told you anything about it. But there is no way you could've known about the liquor I poured on my father's grave."

"He was pretty upset about it."

"Yeah. I could see him being pissed off, which is partly why I did it. He was sort of alcoholic."

"Sort of?"

"Yeah. It's what killed him in the end."

"Is that why he was so—dirty and bloody?"

"He was—what?"

"When I saw him, he was wearing this sweat-stained shirt that had blood on the front."

Jason's mouth pressed into a straight line and the color drained from his cheeks. Charlie winced. She probably should've just kept her mouth shut about such things. It obviously was a shock to hear them.

"I'm sorry. I have a big mouth. You okay?"

"Yeah," Jason said. "It's just weird to hear. That's all. He had gotten drunk and fallen down a brick staircase. I didn't have to ID him, luckily. But I always wondered about it. You know? What did he look like when his neighbor found him? Was he at least dressed?"

"I'm so sorry. I didn't mean to bring you pain."

"No." He shook his head. "It's good to finally know. Thank you."

"So, you never really answered my question."

Jason's lips stretched into a smile. "You want the truth?"

"Truth? Truth is good."

"I found that convenience store. I watched the surveillance video, and I need your help."

"You. You want my help?" Charlie was incredulous.

"Yep. Can you hang here for a minute? I'm just gonna run to my car."

"Sure."

Jason was gone long enough for Charlie to call Jen's house. Her uncle Jack answered, since Jen had to be up at four-thirty in the morning to open her restaurant at six a.m. He insisted she come and stay with them as long as she needed. God love her uncle Jack, he sounded ready to come pack her up and move her in tonight. She assured him it would only be until the lock could be changed. She couldn't wait to close on her condo, then there would be no need to wait on a landlord to change her lock.

She had pulled out her suitcase and started packing when Jason returned carrying several folders. He opened the top one and pulled out the picture of a very pretty young girl, wearing too much makeup. Somewhere deep inside she was glad she had a son and not a daughter. Hopefully it would be easier to keep him a kid longer. It was the girl from her dream.

"Have you ever seen her before?"

"Yes." Charlie's fingers began to tingle and images

flashed through her head. The girl was worried. She was breaking the rules. Lying to her aunt. Maybe she would just get some candy and go home. "She's the girl from my dream. He took her."

"Her aunt reported her missing." Jason's gaze steadied on her.

"She was going to steal some candy, but she didn't because she kept thinking about her aunt." Charlie spoke softly. "What was on the video? Did you see him take her?"

Jason stared down at the photo of the girl. Deep lines cut into his forehead. "Not exactly. It was really strange, actually."

"Strange how?"

"Do you have a DVD player?"

"Sure, in the living room."

Charlie led him to the living room and turned on the television, setting it for the DVD player. Jason pulled the disk from the folder and then from its paper sleeve and handed it to her. After loading it, they sat on her couch, with Jason taking control with the remote. He fast-forwarded through a lot of useless footage until he found the right spot.

"Okay. Just watch this."

The quality of the video surprised her. There, in crisp high-definition, was the man from her dream, pushing the broom around the store. He walked past the girl several times and the discomfort on her face was obvious. The girl picked up a candy bar, stared at it, glanced toward the counter and then brought her gaze back to her hand.

Charlie pointed to the screen. "This is where she's debating with herself about stealing."

"Watch him," Jason said.

Charlie leaned forward with her arms on her knees, unable to look away. The man pushing the broom paused behind the girl, whispering something in her ear before moving forward.

"Do you know what he said?"

Charlie nodded. "He told her to take it."

"But she doesn't."

"No." The skin on Charlie's arms pebbled as she watched the girl put the candy bar back and walk outside. Her heart sped up as the man disappeared from the screen a moment. She almost expected to see herself there, arguing with Aldus Talmadge. The angle of the video changed and Charlie looked to Jason.

"I had our guys edit it a bit. Just watch," he whispered.

From the new angle, Charlie could see the girl on the sidewalk in front of the store, waiting. The man reappeared in the bottom corner, stopping just long enough to say something to his co-worker behind the counter. Charlie's heart jumped to the back of her throat and held its position, threatening to choke her.

Something opaque and white obscured the camera lens and Charlie nearly launched off the couch.

"What happened?" Charlie's voice was too loud and sharp in her ears.

Jason held up a finger. "Just wait." The video reappeared. The girl was gone. The broom pusher walked along the front window as if he was returning from the side parking lot. He pushed open the door, said something to his co-worker and disappeared from view. Jason held up the remote, freezing the frame. "He doesn't make another appearance until four in the morning when he stocks some of the shelves."

"So, we don't really know if he took her or not," Charlie said.

"Oh, I think he took her. I just can't prove it from this," Jason said.

"There were four cameras inside the store—"

"Yep and every single one of them glitched at the same exact time."

"That's crazy."

"Yeah, I think 'statistically impossible' was the term one of our techs used," Jason added. He turned to her, scrutinizing her face. "How did you know there were four cameras?"

"I saw them in my dream," she started. "And I confirmed it when I went there."

"You went there?"

"Uh-huh." She nodded. "He was there. So was my good friend Aldus Talmadge."

"Who?"

"The ghost. I just can't figure out how these two are connected."

"You saw a ghost with this guy?"

"Yep."

"Okay," Jason muttered. She could tell he was still struggling with her ability. "Did he say anything to you?"

"I pretended I couldn't hear him, so he pretty much stopped trying. But he had plenty to say to our mop pusher there."

"Did you hear what he said to him?"

"No." She sighed. "But it wouldn't surprise me if Aldus Talmadge was really behind this girl's disappearance."

Jason didn't respond. Instead he retrieved the DVD, putting it back into its protective sleeve. "It's almost eleven o'clock. Don't want to make your uncle worry."

She gave him a weary smile. "No, we don't want to do that."

CHAPTER 21

Ray Kurtz turned his headlights off and pulled the truck around the ghostly white building to the back parking lot. He glanced into the back of the king cab truck. The jump seats were stowed, and she had nestled in there nicely.

"You stay here," he said.

Her large wet eyes glared at him and she struggled against the plastic ties binding her arms behind her back. The tape covering her mouth muffled the squeaks and cries she made. Didn't she know how beautiful that sound was to him? "I just have to go check something out. I won't be but a minute, promise."

She kicked her bound feet against the jump seat and he frowned.

"Stop that."

She kicked harder.

"If you do it again, I'm gonna smack you hard. I don't want to smack you."

She tried to scream, but the heavy duct tape got in the way. She kicked her feet again. This time hitting the back of his seat. He reached back and grabbed a handful of her hair and slammed her head hard against the back wall of the cab. Two more times and she finally stopped screaming and kicking. Her eyes were half closed. Good. She should sleep. He would wake her up when it came time to be with him one last time.

He brushed his hand over her hair. It was so soft, and it smelled so good when he grabbed her from behind. She was so tiny she barely fought with him at all. That's how he liked it. No struggle. The voice was quiet now. But it would be back to check on him. To make sure he was following the rules.

He got out of the truck, grabbing a shovel and a battery-operated camping lantern from the truck's bed. This far out there were no streetlights, and the darkness wrapped around him like a thick fog until his eyes adjusted to it. He needed to walk across the grave yard, slip over the low brick wall and wait until he couldn't see the back of the church before he dared turn on the light. He was allowed to play with her one last time, but he had to do it in the dark. Ray really hated the dark, but those were the rules of disposal. If he didn't follow the rules, then the dreams started, and the dreams were worse than the dark.

Once it was safe, he turned on the light and waited for the voice to tell him where to go. It was pretty specific.

After several minutes of listening to the sounds of the woods, it spoke—*Head toward the water.*

Ray did as he was told, stopping only when the voice told him to.

Now, dig.

He thrust the sharp edge of the shovel into the soft ground and began to throw the dirt into a mound to make it easier once it came time to cover her up.

* * *

"I AM PERFECTLY CAPABLE OF DRIVING MYSELF," CHARLIE protested.

"You had a blow to the head. You could still have a concussion, Charlie. I'd don't feel comfortable letting you drive this late at night by yourself out on some country road surrounded by water."

"Are you always this ornery and logical?" She folded her arms across her chest.

"Absolutely." He was winning, and he knew it, which pissed her off for reasons she couldn't quite explain.

"It's really late. Don't you have someone at home worrying about where you are?"

"I doubt my cat gives a crap, honestly. Now, who's being ornery?"

She rolled her eyes and shook her head.

"Come on, Charlie, let me drive you. It will make me feel better to know you're safe."

She slipped her hand to her neck and massaged the stiff muscles. Her body ached from her skirmish and her shoulders felt heavy with exhaustion. "Fine," she said. "You win. You can drive."

"Good."

He walked around to the passenger side of his Dodge Charger and opened the door. She slid inside the car, surprised at how comfortable the low bucket seat was. She would have to be careful not to fall asleep. He climbed inside and brought the engine to life with the push of a button.

A few minutes later, they were heading out toward Talmadge Island. Once they were on Maybank highway, the car was plunged into near total darkness.

"You know you can recline if you want, get a little shut eye before we get there." He pushed open the door covering his sunroof. Charlie adjusted her seat and stretched out. It was a clear night. Moonless and this far out from the city the stars were thick pinholes of light against the black velvet sky. She took several deep breaths and let her mind drift. Silence crept up between them. Jason stared straight ahead at the dark road and he gripped the wheel tight with one hand.

"Can I ask you a personal question?"

Charlie opened her eyes and pressed her hand against her belly. Her stomach twisted into a knot and she directed her gaze to him. The question could be one of a thousand things he'd learned about her in his investigation, but her gut told her it would only be one thing. She braced herself. "Sure. You can ask."

"You know I talked to your ex."

"Yeah, I know. He called me."

"It's really none of my business, but I just couldn't stop wondering why you gave up custody of your son. It's a conservative state— from my experience judges tend to like to see children with their mothers."

Relief washed through her. "I didn't give up custody. I still see my son."

"Yeah, I know. I just—"

"Scott and I decided together the best thing for Evan was to make sure his world wasn't completely upended by our divorce. It was just better to keep Evan in his house, at his school, with his friends." She shut her mouth, not willing to say anything more. Hopefully, that would be enough to quell his curiosity about her.

"Oh," Jason said.

"You sound disappointed."

"No." He protested a little too much. "Why should I be?"

She teased him. "Maybe you were hoping for more dirt on me."

"No. Your ex—there was just something about him. He was sort of—"

"Smug? Pompous? A jackass?" Charlie had no problem picturing Scott sitting behind his desk, staring down his nose at Jason.

"Maybe a little of all three." Jason chuckled. "I guess, mainly I wondered what drew you to him, especially since he obviously didn't believe in you."

"Ah." Charlie straightened her seat. "That's easy. He was smart and funny and handsome. What's not to like?"

"Right. Like I said, it's really none of my business."

"If you want to know the truth, we dated our senior year in college and he knew nothing about my...abilities until we'd been married for a couple of years."

"So you what? Sprung it on him?"

"Actually, I had no intention of telling him anything about it, but then I encountered his grandmother in our house right after she died and that sort of outed me. There was this big brouhaha with her children over a ruby ring and she wanted to weigh in."

"Really? Shouldn't she have done that in her will?"

Charlie shrugged. "Yeah, well, sometimes clarity doesn't come till after you die."

"Okay. Good to know. What I don't understand is why your ex still didn't believe you."

"Because Scott doesn't believe in anything except medicine. He figured there was something mentally wrong with me."

"Ah. Is that why you ended up committed at MUSC?"

"You really did your homework, didn't you?"

"I was looking for dirt."

"And you found it." Charlie wanted to be angry, but she wasn't. She understood why he'd gone looking for things to use against her. His need to protect his mother made more sense than ever now that she'd met his father. "No, that's not why. After the whole thing with his grandmother, we just didn't talk about it. It's like there was part of me that he hated and wouldn't even acknowledge. But at the same time, he loved me and wanted to make me happy. We traveled, he showered me with gifts, and we had a baby, but in the end...it wasn't enough."

"I'm sorry." Silence crept up between them again and she only spoke to give him directions. When they finally pulled into her uncle Jack's driveway, they found him sitting in the creaky swing on the back porch. The only light came from inside the kitchen—soft, yellow and inviting.

She loved this house and had spent a lot of time here

as a kid after her parents died. Her uncle Jack was like her second father.

Her uncle stood on the top step, his hulking figure silhouetted by the faint light from the kitchen. At sixty-three, he was done looking the part of trusted doctor. He'd let his salt-and-pepper hair grow out to nearly shoulder length and wore a thick silvery beard to match. If it weren't for his daughter's insistence that he at least dress decently, he might look like a grizzled old mountain man.

"That's your uncle Jack?" Jason asked.

Charlie snickered. Jason barely stood taller than her.

"Yeah. Come on, he's gonna want to meet you."

"Why?" Jason asked.

"You scared?" she teased. A sly grin spread across her lips and she gave him a sideways glance. "If you're scared, just say you're scared."

"I'm not scared." Jason sounded offended.

"Well come on, then."

She stepped onto the gravel drive way and waved. "Hey Uncle Jack."

"Hey there sweet girl." Her Uncle Jack might have looked like he could break a person in half, but he had a voice that put her at ease. "You all right?"

"Yes sir," she said, slowly ascending the steps. Her body had stiffened during the car ride and every muscle in her back and hips ached. "A little sore, but I'm okay."

She got to the top step and stood right in front of him. He tipped her chin up so he could take a better look at the bruise blooming across her cheek. He smiled and brushed his thumb over the butterfly Band-Aids holding the gash on her head together.

"Well, looks like he got you good, huh?" Uncle Jack asked.

"Yeah, he did. I'm hoping you have a heating pad." She rubbed the back of her neck.

"I do," he said. "But a hot Epsom salt bath will probably do more good."

"That sounds marvelous."

Jason trudged up the stairs.

Jack gave him an appraising look. "So you're the young man who's been stalking my niece?"

Even in the dim light, Jason's tan face paled. "No, sir," Jason said cautiously. "I was just looking out for my mother."

"Yeah, and what did you discover?"

Jason glanced from Jack's face to Charlie's. His gaze settled on Charlie's. "Well, it looks like she's the real thing, sir."

"Yeah." Jack smiled at his niece. "She is and she'll do right by you, long as you stop being a jackass."

"Yes, sir," Jason said.

Charlie breathed a sigh of relief, glad that Jason didn't

pull some macho baloney on her uncle. Was it an act? Or was he not letting her uncle ruffle him?

"Well." Jack's gaze settled on Jason. "It's late."

"You go on in, Uncle Jack. I'll be in in a minute."

Her uncle scrutinized her face for a moment then nodded and turned. The screen door squeaked and still managed to slam against the doorframe even with a gentle closing. Charlie crossed her arms and faced Jason.

"Well, I guess you'll be safe here." Jason let his gaze drift over her shoulder to the screen door.

Charlie chuckled. "That's an understatement."

"And you have a ride back to your car in the morning?"

"I do."

Silence swelled between them, enveloping them with awkwardness. Charlie glanced down at her feet and toed the edge of the step. "You know, I didn't thank you for coming to my rescue earlier. So—thank you."

"I'm just glad you're all right. Let me know if you have any more of those dreams about that guy."

"Sure," she said. "Does this mean you're finished investigating me?"

"For now," he teased. He touched her arm giving it a gentle squeeze. "Good night, Charlie."

"Good night, Jason." She fought an overwhelming feeling to hug him. "Drive safe."

"You dream safe." He dug into his back pocket and pulled out a plastic business card case. "I'm serious about calling me." He plucked a single card from the interior sleeve and pressed it into her palm. "My cell number is on the back. Text me if you need me. I'm actually a pretty good listener."

"Thanks," she muttered. She stayed on the porch, watching until he'd gotten in his car and driven away. A cool spring breeze kicked up, wrapping around her and she could smell the river not far off in the distance. At least they weren't at war anymore. Maybe they could even be allies. She could always use another ally.

CHAPTER 22

S ugar tried to sleep but every time she closed her eyes Honey was there. She still hadn't called the psychic. What was she supposed to say? Hello, I'm being haunted by my sister. Do you know how to stop it?

Help me and I will stop.

"I don't know how to help you, Honey. I never have," Sugar said to the room. She glanced around half expecting to find her sister lounging in the rocking chair in the corner. It was empty.

Stop him.

"I don't know who he is." Sugar pushed herself up on her elbows. "How am I supposed to stop him?"

The cell phone on her bedside table lit up. The

number displayed was the psychic's. It began to ring as if she had pressed the Send button.

"Hello?" a sleepy voice said. The heavy breathing didn't sound perverse, more like the person had their mouth perched against the speaker. "Is there someone there?"

Sugar scrambled for the cell phone.

"Yes, hello, I'm here," she said. "I'm so sorry to have called you so late. This is Sugar Blackburn, Susan Tate's mother. She told me I should give you a call. That you had questions."

There was a long pause, but Sugar could hear movement in the background as if the woman was shifting around in her bed.

"Yes. I would like that very much. Would it be possible, though, to do it at some other time? My brain doesn't work very well at three a.m."

"Oh, yes, of course, you're right. I'm so sorry. I should've checked the time." Sugar wasn't quite ready to tell the psychic that her sister had done the dialing. To her knowledge, ghosts had no real sense of time.

"No—no worries. I just had a rough night so—"

"Yes, of course."

"May I call you back in the morning? We can set up a time and I can come see you. I really do better in person for this sort of thing."

"Certainly. That makes total sense."

"Great," she yawned. "My name is Charlie, by the way."

"It's very nice to meet you, Charlie."

"Nice to meet you too."

"I'll talk to you in the morning, then."

"Yes," Charlie said sleepily. "In the morning."

Sugar pressed the red phone icon and turned to the room. "Are you happy now?"

The rocking chair in the corner began to rock slowly back and forth.

Sugar glared at the empty rocker. "Honey, you need to leave."

The chair began to rock harder. Sugar scowled as she grabbed her pillow and the afghan from the end of her bed. She didn't look at the rocker again as she headed into her living room to sleep on the couch. She was done dealing with ghosts tonight.

"OH, LOOK, IT'S DEPUTY DOGGED." LISA PULLED INTO AN empty space at Summerfield Retirement Community and put her BMW in park. Charlie had brought her cousin as back-up Friday afternoon. What she didn't expect was Jason Tate waiting on the sidewalk for them. He wore mirrored sunglasses, a fitted pair of faded jeans and a tight blue T-shirt, showing the cut of his chest and biceps. The scruff on his face had been shaven clean.

"You be nice," Charlie said.

"What? I'm always nice," Lisa quipped, "And, anyway, he's not my boyfriend, he's yours."

"He is not my boyfriend."

"You're right. He just showed up and rescued you for no reason."

"He did not rescue me!" Charlie's face burned, and she tried to ignore Lisa's yeah-right look. "And he is not my boyfriend, so just cut it out."

"What? He's cute and at least he seems to have accepted your unique abilities."

"You're impossible, you know that?"

"Uh-huh."

"Hey," Jason said, approaching the car.

"Hey, I didn't expect to see you here." Charlie couldn't stop the smile spreading across her face.

"My grandmother called and asked me to come. How you doing?"

"Much better, thank you. I took it easy yesterday and got a good night's sleep." Charlie bit back a smile. There was no need to give Lisa any more ammo to use against her. "Just so you know, there was no concussion."

"Well, that's good news." Jason clapped his hands and rubbed them together. "So, you ready to go commune with the dead?"

Lisa scowled and gave Charlie a what-the-hell look, but she just laughed. It was good they could joke about it.

"Lead the way," Charlie said. They followed him into the lobby and the cool, stale air slapped them in the face. The scent of citrus air freshener coated the back of Charlie's throat but beneath that smell was something else. Something more human—feces, urine, and even the sickly sweetness of death lingered in the undercurrent, reminding her this is where they sent the old to die.

The floral pattern of dark burgundy carpeting reminded Charlie of her granny's house. She'd had an area rug in her dining room with a similar design. Her granny had once told her floral patterns were good for covering any number of stain sins. From food to blood. Once it was cleaned up, it just mixed right in with the pattern.

They walked through the building and Charlie nodded and greeted every person she saw. Lisa stuck nearby. She was never one to particularly like old people or very young people, which was why she had no children of her own at nearly thirty-five.

Charlie, on the other hand, liked them all—young and old. Maybe it was just the customer service rep in her, but she thought that every person had something to offer and deserved to be heard. And everybody deserved to be treated with respect.

Lisa wrapped her hand tightly around her purse strap

and her knuckles whitened. "Feels like they're all about to die. Do you sense that?"

Charlie shook her head. "Not exactly."

"He's hovering close, though."

"Who's hovering?" Jason stuck his head between the two of them.

Lisa looked him in the eye. "Death."

"All right, you two need to stop taking yourselves so serious."

"Just because you don't sense him, doesn't mean he isn't real," Lisa said.

Jason scowled. "Come on, her apartment's around the corner. She likes to sit on the porch in the afternoon and cat-call the golfers."

"Sounds like my kind of old person," Lisa said under her breath. Charlie bit the inside of her cheek, fighting back a grin.

Jason stopped at number 173. He knocked and turned the knob at the same time. "Gran? You here?"

Something jerked the door open, and it slammed against the wall. Charlie felt the spirit of the girl immediately, but didn't see her.

"Oh-kay, that was weird," Jason murmured. He took a step forward but something stopped him. His hand went to his throat and his face reddened.

"Jason?" Alarm rang through Charlie's chest and she pulled him back into the hallway. His chest heaved, and he coughed. He doubled-over with his hands on his knees sucking in large breaths.

"What the hell?" he said between gasps for air. His eyes frantically searched the empty doorway.

"Lisa," Charlie said.

"It's fine, I've got him. You go." Lisa gently touched Jason's back. "How 'bout we go find some place to sit while Charlie works?"

"What was that?" He straightened up and rubbed his throat.

"I'll explain everything. Come on." Lisa guided him back toward the lobby.

Charlie took a step into the apartment waiting to see if she would suffer the same fate as Jason. Something yanked her forward, and the hinge creaked as the door closed. The lock clicked and Charlie's heart sped up.

"Mrs. Blackburn? Are you here?" Charlie called. The small apartment consisted of a well-appointed living room and a small kitchen. The pretty floral couch and coordinating chairs faced a media cabinet with a large flat screen TV hanging on the wall above it. "Mrs. Blackburn?"

Charlie pulled her phone from her back pocket and checked the time. They were supposed to meet at two p.m.

"She's not here," a gravelly voice came from behind her. Charlie slowly turned. Her heart beat hard against her ribs as she came face-to-face with a teenage girl—or at least she had been in life.

"Who are you?" Charlie asked, taking in the girl's appearance. Her long hair was caked with mud and dark bruises stained the nearly translucent skin around her neck. The red and black of her eyes disturbed Charlie the most. She could not tell what color the girl's eyes had been when she lived. Perhaps they were hazel like Jason's or dark brown like Susan's. It was hard to know.

"Can you help me?" the girl asked.

"I'll try," Charlie said. "Can you tell me your name?"

"Honey Talmadge."

Charlie offered a wan smile. "My name is Charlie. You're Ms. Blackburn's sister, the one she told me about. Right?"

"Yes." The girl's voice quivered. "She married Frank. She thought she could leave me behind."

The girl let out a groan that morphed into a bloodcurdling keening. So much pain in that sound. It made Charlie's bones ache. She pressed her hands against her ears. "Honey—I know it hurts. But I can't help you if you're screaming."

The girl closed her mouth and fixed her stare on Charlie. Her lip quivered, but she did not cry again.

"That's better. Was Frank your boyfriend?"

"No, of course not. He was too young for me. But he took my sister away."

"I'm sorry that happened. Honey, can you tell me how I can help you?"

"You have to stop him."

"Who?"

"Talmadge. You must stop him."

"You mean Aldus Talmadge?"

Girl nodded her head. "He won't stop collecting them."

"Is that what he's doing? Collecting the girls? How is he collecting them? How do I stop him?"

The jiggling of the door handle drew Charlie's attention. She didn't want to look away. She wanted answers. Muffled voices came from the hall.

"Honey. Please. Tell me," Charlie whispered. The door opened behind her and the ghost disappeared.

"Thank you, Henry."

Charlie recognized the old woman's voice from their phone conversation. She took a deep breath and turned to greet Sugar Blackburn.

"Ms. Blackburn? Do you know this woman? Should I call security?" An older man wearing gray coveralls appraised Charlie with wary eyes.

"Charlie?" Sugar asked.

Charlie called up a smile. "Yes, ma'am."

"I'm so sorry I'm late." Sugar carried a plastic basket with neatly folded clothes. "There was a problem with the dryers."

"No worries. I hope you don't mind that I let myself in."

"Oh, no, of course not. I thought Jason was coming with you."

"He did. He just—" Charlie's gaze shifted to the man in the coveralls lingering behind Sugar. "He needed some fresh air."

Sugar's sharp, hazel eyes scanned the room. "I see." Sugar turned to the man. "Thank you again for all your help, Henry."

Henry nodded and gave Charlie an uncertain glance before heading down the hall out of sight. Sugar put the basket down and closed the door behind her.

"Are you all right?" Sugar asked.

"I am. I met your sister."

"She showed herself to you?"

Charlie nodded. "She's in a lot of pain."

"I don't understand. She's dead. How can she be in pain?"

Charlie sighed. "Sometimes spirits hold onto emotions for people and things. It's one way they bind themselves to this world."

Sugar covered her mouth with her hand and her eyes became glassy. "Poor Honey."

"Can you tell me more about how she died?"

"Of course, I'll tell you anything you want if it will help her find some peace."

CHAPTER 23

Charlie leaned her head against the window of Lisa's BMW and watched the world blur by. Sometimes when she listened to people's stories, images popped into her head—like a movie— only what she saw was their thoughts. It wore her out, especially when there was pain involved. Listening to Sugar's story left her feeling raw and exposed. The poor woman had been haunted by her sister for nearly seventy years. In all that time, she had relived that night over and over. Charlie admired her for her strength. She wasn't sure she could have dealt with it as graciously. Hell, she could barely deal with her marriage imploding. There was no way she would've been able to handle it if her dead sister had made a habit of showing up to make her feel bad for not doing more to help her.

"Are you all right?" Lisa asked.

"I'm fine," Charlie said. "I just keep thinking about Honey's story."

"Yeah," Lisa said. "It's really sad."

"You know, Sugar told me that the man who killed her claimed he was told to do it by a voice in his head. They still electrocuted him though."

"Well, of course, they did. It was the forties, right?"

"Yeah, I think so." Charlie nodded. "But, it's not just Honey who's on my mind."

"What do you mean?"

"I keep having this dream. It's about a young girl—a worker. It's like I've stepped inside a historical movie or something. She's young and black, working on a potato farm."

"What happens to her?"

"She dies at the hands of Aldus Talmadge."

"Aldus Talmadge," Lisa practically spat his name. "I wish that SOB would just cross on over to hell."

"Me, too. I know Susan's counting on me, but I don't know how to make him go."

"Maybe we should all put our heads together," Lisa said. "Call a family meeting. I'm sure Jen and Daphne will have some ideas."

"At this point, I'll take all the help I can get. There's something I can't figure out."

"What?" Lisa's hands tightened around the polished wood of her steering wheel and her knuckles whitened.

"Honey told me Talmadge is collecting girls."

"The ones you saw in the woods?"

"I guess. I just...I'm not sure exactly how he's collecting them."

Lisa shrugged. "Maybe you should go talk to them."

Charlie groaned. "I don't want to go back until I know how to get rid of him."

"Yeah, but what if the only way you can get rid of him is by talking to them?"

"Damn you and your logical brain." Charlie's phone buzzed in her hand and she flipped it over and glanced at the screen. "Sorry. This is my realtor."

Lisa flashed her a hopeful look. "Did you get it?"

"I don't know yet. We've been going back and forth with offers." Charlie pressed the red phone icon with her thumb. "Hi, Evelyn."

"Hi, Charlie."

"Any news?"

"Well, do you want the good news or the bad news first?" The woman's cautious tone caused panic to flutter in Charlie's chest.

"What's wrong?" Charlie braced herself.

"Well, honey, I'm sorry to have to break this to you but another buyer outbid you."

"What?" Charlie clenched her jaw. Great. This was

just exactly what she needed on top of everything else. "I really need to get into a place of my own."

"I know, I know, and I'm so sorry." Evelyn's voice oozed regret. "The good news is I have a few other listings that meet your criteria that you haven't seen yet."

"So, we have to start over," Charlie muttered. "Maybe this is a sign."

"Nonsense." Evelyn turned upbeat. "I promise we will get you into a house or a condo or something. I am on top of this, and I promise you, Charlie, we will find you the perfect place to live." Evelyn's can-do spirit could be grating but at the moment Charlie was grateful, because it meant Evelyn's attention would be focused. Charlie just didn't know when she would find time to look at houses with everything else that was going on.

"I appreciate that, Evelyn. Just call me when you have some information."

"I sure will. I am pouring over the MLS as we speak."

"Great. Thanks." Charlie pressed End and sat back with her head against the headrest.

Lisa looked over at her. "Well, that didn't sound good."

"I was outbid," Charlie said dully.

"Oh, honey, I'm so sorry." Lisa patted her cousin's arm. "I'm sure something will come up."

"I really, really hope so. I don't really feel safe going back to my apartment, even once the locks are changed."

Lisa sighed, and they drove the rest of the way back to Palmetto Point in silence.

* * *

THE BLUE-HAIRED YOUNG WOMAN APPROACHED THEIR table. "You want another glass of tea?" Charlie glanced at her nametag. She could never remember the girl's name. Charlie smiled.

"Thank you, that'd be great." The young woman picked up her glass and poured in more tea and ice. Charlie watched her walk away, letting her gaze scan across her cousin's busy diner. She had decided to take Lisa's advice to talk to Jen about her confusion with the case. She'd stopped in for a few minutes before heading out to pick up Evan for their weekend together.

Jen was behind the counter talking to the evening manager, giving her last-minute instructions. Poor Jen had already been here since four-thirty this morning, and it was going on four p.m. now. Charlie had no idea how Jen did it six days a week. Of course, maybe that's why she was so successful. Sometimes Charlie wished she could find something to dedicate her life and energy to. Something she loved as much as Jen loved this restaurant. A pang of jealousy wound around her heart and she hated herself a little for it.

Finally, Jen untied her apron, slipped it over her head,

and shoved it into a cubby beneath the register. When she approached Charlie's table a wide smile was painted across her face.

"Sorry about that," Jen said pushing into the seat across from Charlie.

"No problem, Jen. It's great that y'all are so busy here."

"I know. I can't believe how much we've grown." Jen leveled her gaze on Charlie. "You know I am so happy you and Evan are spending the weekend at the house. Ruby hasn't stopped talking about it since I told her. She just loves her cousin Evan."

Charlie smiled. "Evan adores her." Charlie picked up her glass and took a sip of tea, trying to figure out how to bring up her question.

The blue-haired waitress walked over. "Can I get you anything, ma'am?"

Jen rolled her blue eyes. "Arden, will you just bring me a piece of pie?"

"Of course—ma'am." A grin playing at the corners of Arden's mouth as she teased her boss. "What sort of pie would you like? We have several varieties."

"Just bring me piece of the chocolate pie with two forks."

"Yes, ma'am," Arden said, writing it down on her pad before she walked away.

"We've been working on her manners with

customers," Jen explained.

Charlie tried to suppress a smile. "I see that. Looks like she still needs some work."

"Yeah, no kidding. If she wasn't Ellen's daughter, I wouldn't have hired her, but you know how those things go." Jen sighed.

"Yeah, especially in a town like this." Charlie nodded.

Jen leaned forward with her arms on the table. She laced her fingers together and steadied her gaze on Charlie. "You know, I like having you at the house. So does daddy, by the way."

"Come on, it's only been a couple of days. And I've been nothing but a royal pain in the ass. It was almost midnight when I got there Wednesday night, and then your father insisted on redoing my bandages."

"I know, but he loves having you. He thinks of you and Daphne as his other daughters. and you know how he feels about his daughters."

"I do." Charlie traced the rim of her glass. Her Uncle Jack liked having his girls close. "Once I go home, I'll try to do better about coming around for Friday dinners and stuff."

"Lisa said you lost the condo." Jen kept her eyes on her, unwavering.

"Lisa has a big mouth." Charlie chuckled.

"Well, that's beside the point. But it means you don't have a place to live."

"I still have a place to live."

"I mean a safe place to live."

"My landlord is changing the locks on Monday, and since the intruder didn't try to steal anything—"

"What if I gave you an alternate solution?"

"Jen—"

"How about you move into the cottage? Rent-free."

"No." Charlie sat back hard against the booth. "No. That's crazy."

"Why?" Jen asked. "It's not the main house, so you'll still have your privacy. You know the property has protections in place, and it has two bedrooms so there's a place for Evan when he comes to visit on weekends. It's perfect. Plus, I'll get to see you more. And I'll know you're safe."

"I thought Uncle Jack was gonna turn that cottage into a man cave. You know, to get away from all the estrogen in your house."

Jen laughed out loud. "My father loves all the estrogen in his house and couldn't live without it. And he always has his boat if he really needs a break."

Charlie quirked an eyebrow at her cousin. "Really? That doesn't put a damper on your love life?" Charlie smirked and for a moment it felt like they were in high school again. "What happens when you meet a boy?"

"Who has time for boys?" Jen snorted. She patted Charlie's hand. "We'll jump off that bridge when we get to it. In the meantime, I couldn't have this restaurant and live my dream if it weren't for my dad helping me take care of Ruby." Jen's blue eyes softened. "He loves you, Charlie, and he just wants to take care of you."

"I love him, too, but I don't need him to take care of me. If I wanted to be taken care of, I could've just stayed married."

"No, you couldn't have. Don't get me wrong. I like Scott. He's a great dad, and I know that he still cares for you deeply, but he was never going to fully accept who you are."

"Who I am?" Charlie scoffed. "Nobody deserves this kind of crazy. Truly. If I learned anything being married, it was that."

"You know it burns me up sometimes how much Scott is still in your head. What you have is a calling, really. A blessing."

Charlie fiddled with the saltshaker, spinning it in a circle between her thumb and forefinger. "It's more curse than blessing. I've spent the better part of my adult life trying to ignore it."

"I know. And it almost killed you—literally."

Charlie met her cousin's unwavering gaze. How was she supposed to respond to that? There was no denying that trying to be who Scott thought she should be had led to her depression and the ultimate destruction of her marriage, but she didn't quite know how to be as comfortable in her own skin as Jen was. She envied Jen's total acceptance of herself.

Jen's phone buzzed in her bag. She pulled it out and glanced at the screen. "Okay. Lisa says Jason is on TV."

"What?" Charlie asked.

Jen got to her feet. "Come on. Hurry."

Charlie followed her cousin into the back kitchen where she had a tiny office. Evangeline had already left for the day. A small flat screen television hung on the wall above the desk. Jen picked up the remote and clicked the power button. They barely caught the tail end of an interview with Sergeant Jason Tate.

"He's cute," Jen said. Charlie threw a 'whatever' look at her cousin and continued to watch.

"Yes, ma'am. If anyone has any information, they should call the police at this number." Jason looked at the reporter instead of the camera.

An 800-number flashed across the screen in bright red. The reporter turned back to the camera.

"This is the second young woman to go missing in less than ten days." The reporter used her smooth reporting voice. "The police could use any leads on finding these two girls. It's believed they've been taken by the same man."

Two photos of two different girls appeared on the screen, followed by a still shot of black and white security footage.

Charlie cursed under her breath.

"What is it?"

"That's the guy from the gas station, the one I dreamed about. The one I saw with Aldus Talmadge."

"You're sure?"

"Yeah, I'm sure."

"Do you know if they're alive?"

Charlie squeezed her eyes shut and concentrated on their faces. She just wanted something, some sign that there was still hope. She clenched her teeth and growled before blowing out a heavy breath. "I can't tell. I need more of a connection." Charlie glanced at the clock on the wall. "Hey, I have to pick up Evan. Any chance you could take care of him for me for a little while? There's something I need to do."

"What?"

"Honey Talmadge told me I had to stop him from collecting."

"Collecting what?"

"Girls." Charlie pointed to the television, even though the newscasters had moved onto a different story.

"How is he doing that? He's dead."

"Yeah, he is—but I don't think that made him less powerful."

"What do you mean?"

"Sugar told me that the Talmadge's once owned property on the other islands as well as Talmadge Island.

I think he's moving in the boundaries of their old property lines because in his mind he still owns it. That convenience store is right over the bridge from Talmadge Island. How much you want to bet the property it's on once belonged to the Talmadges."

"But then how did he go to your apartment?"

"Maybe he attached himself to me and followed me home."

"What are you gonna do?"

"I'm gonna suck it up and go talk to the girls in the woods. I think that's what Honey meant. They're the ones he's been collecting. Hopefully, they can tell me something."

"You're not going alone."

"I don't think they'll talk to me if I'm with someone else. I'll be fine."

"Dang it, Charlie." Jen frowned and pulled a bag from a large file drawer in the desk. "I was gonna give these out when we all went over there together." She pulled a taupe linen bag from the large tote and pushed it toward Charlie.

"What's this?"

"Every tool I have in my arsenal for dealing with evil spirits. I made a bag for each of us. You know for cleansing the house."

Charlie untied the brown grosgrain ribbon holding the bag closed and reached inside. Her fingers brushed against a velvet box and she pulled it from the bag first. Charlie flipped open the top and the burnished silver pendant winked at her in the overhead light of the office. "Is this what I think it is?"

"Yep. It's for a little added protection."

"You know people are gonna start to think we're witches," Charlie teased, brushing her thumb over the five-sided star.

Jen shrugged one shoulder. "Half the town already knows, and the other half suspects."

"But I'm not a witch."

"You could be." Jen reached for the box and removed the necklace. "If you'd just embrace your heritage."

Charlie sighed. They'd had this discussion too many times.

"Fine, I'll let it go...for now," Jen said. "Turn around."

Charlie bent low and Jen fastened the second necklace around her neck. The pendant dropped into Charlie's pale pink T-shirt, out of sight.

"There. That's the best I've got to give, along with the stuff in your bag."

Charlie quirked one eyebrow. "Which is what?"

"A sage bundle for smudging, a bag of salt mixed with dried sage. A small piece of sandalwood, a pocketknife and some matches in a plastic bag. Just in case."

"I'm just going to talk with them. I'm not camping out with them," Charlie quipped.

"Yeah, well, it can't hurt. There are also a few loose stones and crystals."

"You know I have no affinity for magic like you do, Jen. The sandalwood, sage, and salt I can use, but the crystals—I have no idea how to harness them."

"When the time comes, reach inside the pouch without looking. Let your intuition guide you. It won't steer you wrong. Once you've picked a stone, call on a spirit guide to help you."

"A spirit guide? Really?" Charlie tried not to let too much skepticism show in her face, but she knew she failed when Jen frowned and rolled her eyes.

"Yes, really. You can't go into this halfway. It could get you seriously hurt, or worse."

"Jen—"

"I'm not kidding about this Charlie. He's already proven he can physically hurt you. So, watch your back and don't be afraid to be who you are. It's your birthright."

There was no point in arguing with her cousin. Lisa might be the lawyer, but Jen was the most persuasive of them all when it came down to it. She knew exactly how to use her truth to hit a person in the heart.

"I'll be careful," Charlie said, tucking the bag into her purse. She hugged her cousin tight and left before she could change her mind.

CHAPTER 24

E van was waiting on the front porch hugging a backpack to his chest when Charlie arrived late Friday afternoon. His face lit up, and he jumped to his feet and ran down the steps.

"Mom!" he said.

Charlie slammed her car into park, jumped out, and had her arms wrapped around him before Scott could argue about her display of affection on the front lawn where the neighbors could see. She picked him up and swung him around.

Setting him down, she stepped back and took a long look at him. "I swear you're two inches taller since I saw you two days ago."

Evan laughed. "I haven't grown that fast, Mom."

"Well, you're gonna be tall like your mama." *Thank*

goodness, she added silently. She ruffled his fine blond hair. Evan was a perfect mix of her and Scott. He had her blue eyes and Scott's lips and square jaw. The only thing questionable was his nose—looking at him straight on it appeared to be hers, long, thin, and straight. But in profile, it was all Scott, even down to the curve of the tip of his nose.. "You ready to go have some fun?"

"Yeah," he said.

"Okay, go get in the car. I need to talk to your daddy for a second." She cast her gaze over to the front porch where Scott now stood with his hands in his pockets. She walked to the bottom of the steps, not wanting to get too close. She'd covered the bruise on her jaw with makeup and had arranged her bangs over the cut on her forehead to make them less noticeable, but she couldn't cover her split lip very well.

"I'll have him back by early Sunday evening," she said.

"All right." He tipped his chin to the right and his eyebrows tugged together as if he was questioning something. Her heartbeat quickened, and she sucked her bottom lip into her mouth. Any concern at all and he could stop her from seeing her son, regardless of their agreement. All he had to do was call one of his judge friends. He opened his mouth to say something, and she glanced back at the car. Evan stood in the doorframe of the passenger side with his arms over the roof of the car.

"Come on, Mom, let's go," he said.

"I'm coming."

"We have supper at six o'clock on Sundays," Scott said. It was not an invitation. More of a warning.

"I remember." Charlie took a step backwards.

"Evan listen to your mom now. You hear me?" Scott called.

"Yes, sir."

Charlie rushed to the car, not looking back. She climbed into the driver seat and Evan climbed into the passenger seat.

"Phew, that was a close call," she said to Evan.

"Mom," Evan said, "what happened your face?"

"I got into an accident, sweetie. Can you believe it? I fell up the steps in the townhouse." She didn't look at him as she lied. That would have made it harder.

"Wow, that must've hurt." His gaze bounced from the gash on her forehead to the bruise on her cheek, to the split in her lip. He scrutinized her for another moment before finally saying, "I'm glad you're all right."

"Me too, sweetie," she said.

"So, did you have the locks changed?"

Busted. She didn't know why she thought she could lie to him just because he was young. Of all the things he'd inherited from her, his sensitivity and intuition were just as much a part of him as his blond hair.

"I put a request in with maintenance at the apartment

building, so you and I are actually not going to be staying at my apartment this weekend."

"Where are we staying?"

"Uncle Jack's. Won't that be fun? He's taking you and Ruby fishing in the morning."

"Cool. I love Uncle Jack. He's the most fun."

"Yes, he is." Charlie grinned. "We should get going. I've got an errand I need to run, so, back seat buddy." She jerked her thumb toward the rear seat.

"Aw, Mom, I'm almost eleven."

"You know the rules."

Evan frowned. "Fine." He opened the car door and crawled into the back seat. They buckled up, and she gave Scott a short wave before putting the car in reverse and backing out into the street.

"By the way, I'm not gonna be there for supper, but the rest of the family will be."

"What kind of errand?"

"Oh, just something I need to do for work. I'll be home in time to tuck you in, though. Okay?" She glanced at him in the rearview mirror.

Evan stared at his mother for a long moment. A worry line appeared between his eyebrows. "Okay. Just promise you'll be careful."

Charlie smiled at her wise child. "I will, baby. I promise."

CHAPTER 25

Charlie put her car in park and peered through her windshield at the darkened house. It appeared Susan wasn't home, but Charlie didn't think it would matter to her if she spoke to the spirits in the woods. It was, after all, what she'd been asked to do.

In the distance thunder rumbled and dark clouds gathered over the marsh. She would have to hurry if she didn't want to be rained on. Charlie slung the small canvas messenger bag across her body and tucked her keys inside one of the zippered compartments. She popped the trunk and dug around the emergency box that Scott made her keep. Her fingers brushed against cold metal and she wrapped her hand around the flashlight. Pressing the silver button, she tested it. The light shined bright and strong. It was nearly seven and it wouldn't be dark for at least another hour, but it was better to be safe than sorry. She closed her trunk and slipped the light inside her bag.

Out of politeness, she climbed the stairs and knocked on the front door. "Susan?"

There was no answer. Charlie peeked inside the window and all the lights were off. No sign of life. Maybe that was a good thing.

She headed around back, and one by one the apparitions appeared in the tree line. Her heart quickened at the sight of them. It wasn't exactly fear she felt. There was no danger emanating from them, only sadness. A despair that connected with something deep inside of her. She had felt it before. The night she OD'd on sleeping pills and nearly died. She had clawed her way back from the darkness, somehow finding the will to live again. If she feared anything, it was the transfer of their misery onto her. When she was finished learning what she could from them, would she be able to just walk away and shake off the inevitable anguish she was sure to feel? Her hand found the silver pentacle, and she pressed her thumb hard against the star, letting it leave a deep imprint in her skin. She took a deep breath and headed for the woods.

* * *

Honey just would not leave her alone. Sugar
thought that once her dead sister realized she had done
all she could to help that maybe Honey could pass on to
wherever it was she was supposed to go. Sugar wasn't sure
if she believed in heaven anymore, and if hell existed
then more than likely, it was on this plane not another.

The rocking chair in her bedroom had not stopped
moving since Honey decided to move in and make her
presence known. Back and forth. Back and forth. The old
wood creaked, grating Sugar's last nerve. She sighed and
tried to focus on the letters needed for the latest puzzle
on Wheel of Fortune. The young woman spinning the
wheel had just won nearly $7000. She hoped she
wouldn't get tripped up on the bonus round. That was
always the hardest. Sugar almost never guessed the
bonus round correctly.

The creaking stopped, making Sugar look over to the
bedroom door. Maybe Honey had left. She could hope
anyway.

An icy finger brushed across the back of her neck.
There was a whoosh of cold air and a slight popping
sound. Sugar sighed.

"Honey, it is time for you to go." Sugar faced her sister
and found the ghost so close their noses almost touched.

"Help her," Honey said.

"Honey I have done all I can to help." Sugar scooted
to her left putting some space between them.

"Help her," Honey repeated.

"I have done everything you've asked. Why don't you just leave me in peace?"

Honey's face darkened. "Help her."

The cell phone sitting on the end table began to ring and Sugar picked it up.

Charlie Payne's number appeared. It took Sugar a moment to realize Charlie wasn't calling her. Honey had dialed Charlie's phone again.

"Hello, you've reached my cell phone. Leave me a message and I will call you back as soon as I can. You have a great day now," Charlie's voice mail message said in her calm steady voice.

"Charlie, this is Sugar Blackburn. I was just calling to make sure you're all right. Can you please give me a call when you get this? Thank you."

Sugar tapped End and glared at her sister's apparition. "Is there anything else you'd like me to do tonight? Because honestly? Jeopardy starts in about five minutes, and I'm not gonna pay you any attention once it starts."

The speed of her sister's movement didn't quite register until fear clogged her throat. Honey's cold hands wrapped around Sugar's neck squeezing just enough to feel the pressure of her icy fingertips

"Honey," Sugar whispered. "Please don't."

"Help her," Honey's ragged voice snaked through

Sugar's senses making her bones ache.

"Let me go."

Something sharp bit into her skin and Honey's grip tightened for a brief second, cutting off Sugar's air before releasing. Sugar's hand went to her neck, and she sucked in a deep breath. Her fingertips met with something warm and sticky. Sugar drew her fingers back and found them smeared with blood.

"All right, you've made your point," Sugar said. "What do you want me to do? And don't say help her. That's not helpful."

The phone began to ring again. Sugar frowned and glanced screen. Her grandson's number displayed with a picture of the two of them. Sugar put her ear to the phone, listening to it ring.

"Hey, Gran," Jason said. "Can I call you back? I'm kinda in the middle of something."

"Jason—we have to help Charlie." Sugar moved into the bathroom to find the source of blood. She leaned in close to see four thin crescent-shaped wounds on the side of her neck.

Jason cleared his throat. "Why do you say that, Gran?"

Sugar put the phone on speaker and took a clean washcloth from the top drawer. She ran it under cold water, wrung it out, and touched it to her neck. When she glanced into the large mirror over the sink, Honey appeared, her black eyes watching Sugar's every move. "I have it on good authority that she needs help. I tried calling her, but all I got was her voice mail."

"That just means she's not answering her phone, Gran. I'm sure she's fine."

Sugar blinked and when she opened her eyes again, Honey had moved behind her. The air chilled, and a tremor skittered down Sugar's spine. Air escaped Sugar's lips, puffing in a slow visible stream. "Well, I'm not sure she is."

"Listen, Gran I don't want you to worry about it. I've got to go. Love you."

"Jason," she started, but the phone clicked. She glanced at the screen and the end time blinked at her before disappearing. "Well, that little devil hung up on me."

Honey touched a cold finger to Sugar's cheek.

"What am I supposed to do, Honey? Just tell me what to do." She said the words as if she were a thirteen-year-old girl again looking to her big sister for advice. A pang of sadness squeezed her heart. How she missed those times.

"Go home, Sugar. Go home," the ragged whisper flitted across her skin, echoing through her head and her sister faded to mist.

CHAPTER 26

J ason curled his fingers into a fist and raised his hand to knock against the screen door. There were several cars parked behind Charlie's uncle's house, but he didn't see her blue Honda. She'd ridden to meet his grandmother with her cousin, though, so maybe she still didn't have her car. He'd forgotten to ask if her landlord had changed her locks. He wasn't even sure why he thought she could help, other than something in his gut told him she could and he wasn't going to start doubting his instincts.

He heard a woman talking in a hushed tone. "I don't have a good feeling about this, Jen. We should not have let her go out there by herself. You said yourself this spirit is dangerous." Jason stepped to the right, which gave him a view of the kitchen but kept him out of sight.

Two women entered the kitchen carrying dishes. One was much older, with long white hair that reached the middle of her back. The other was younger, closer to Charlie's age, with short dark hair and a face like a pixie.

"Charlie is a grown woman. I can't make her do something she doesn't want to do."

"Still, I don't like it." The older woman picked up the plates and scraped the bits of leftover food into the trash before placing each dish into the sink. The sound of the metal fork against the porcelain set his teeth on edge.

"She'll be fine. She's just going to talk to the other spirits on the property. I doubt Talmadge will even be there. And, anyway, Charlie has her phone. She can call if she needs us," the younger woman said. "Have a little faith."

"Will you get the pie out of the fridge, please?" The older woman opened a cabinet and pulled out a stack of small plates.

"Sure," the younger woman said.

Jason stepped up to the door and rapped his knuckles against the painted wood. The younger woman appeared at the screen door.

"Jason Tate," she said, smiling as if she knew him.

"Um. Hi," he said. Maybe Charlie wasn't the only special one in her family. "Is Charlie here?"

"Come on in. Would you like a piece of pie?" The

young woman pulled the screen door open and ushered him inside.

"Hello." The older woman turned to him. In her hand, she held a pie server with chocolate clinging to its blade.

"Thank you, but, no. I was just looking for Charlie. I tried calling her, but she's not answering her cell phone, and I remember her saying something about Friday night dinner with her family." Jason's gaze bounced between the two women. Charlie's Uncle Jack may have been the guard dog of the family, but clearly these two were the gatekeepers. He got the feeling no one passed into their inner sanctum without their permission.

"She's not answering her phone?" The older woman gave the younger woman a pointed look.

"No, ma'am, it goes straight to voice mail," he said. "I thought maybe she'd turned it off."

"I'm Jen, by the way." The younger woman stepped forward and offered her hand. "Charlie's cousin."

"Nice to meet you." He shook her hand and smiled. "Charlie sure has a lot of cousins."

"Indeed, she does young man," the older woman said. She gave him the once over. "I'm Evangeline Ferebee, her aunt."

"It's nice to meet you, ma'am." He recognized the last name. Jason tried to keep from cringing. "Daphne's mother?"

"That's correct." Her mouth twisted with disapproval. He wondered what Daphne had said.

"So...Charlie's not here?"

The women exchanged glances again, and he got the feeling there was something more than the mutual looks passing between them.

The older woman's mouth twisted into a scowl. "You may as well tell him."

"Charlie went to your mother's house," Jen said.

"My mother's in Savannah till Sunday. Why did she go out there?"

"She wanted to talk to some of the spirits out there," Jen said.

The matter-of-factness of her statement still shocked him, despite his first-hand experience earlier in the day. His neck twitched from muscle memory and he could almost feel the invisible hands cutting off his access to air again. He rubbed his throat. "Is that safe?" he asked.

The two women responded simultaneously.

"No," Evangeline said.

"Yes," Jen countered.

The women looked at each other and frowned.

Jen sighed. "Charlie's been talking to spirits a long time. I have no doubt she's fine."

"Hello, deputy," Lisa said as she walked into the kitchen carrying more dirty dishes. She put them in the sink and leaned against the counter. "This is a surprise."

"Hi, Lisa." He offered her a perfunctory smile.

"Charlie's not answering her cell phone," Evangeline said.

Lisa's gaze bounced from her aunt to Jen to Jason. "Uh, should we be worried?"

"I think we should," Evangeline said quietly. Jen and Lisa shifted their gaze toward each other and Lisa's head began to bob in a nod.

"Fine. I give in," Jen relented. "Evangeline, can you watch Ruby and Evan?"

"Of course," Evangeline said.

"Lisa, get Daphne. I'll get the bags and we'll go do our thing."

"Wait. What's happening?" Jason held his hands up, unsure how his simple request to talk to Charlie had moved into some sort of action.

"You go get the bags. I'll fill him in." Lisa folded her arms across her chest and stepped forward. Jen nodded and disappeared through the swinging door. "Listen, Charlie thinks that this spirit guy is tied to the girls who have gone missing."

"What? How?"

"Charlie met with more than just your grandmother today. She talked with Honey Talmadge. I guess, she'd have been your great aunt if she'd lived."

"Okay—" Jason listened carefully, trying to keep himself from jumping to any conclusions or scoffing at the impossibility of Lisa's words. He didn't have the luxury of skepticism anymore. "And what did Honey have to say?"

"You know, it's a really long story. One that I'd be happy to tell you on the way there."

CHAPTER 27

The gloom of the woods made it difficult to see, even with the dying light of the day filtering through. As Charlie approached, the girls' apparitions began to disappear. She hoped once she showed herself to be friendly, they would come back. She clicked on the flashlight. She had walked deep enough into the dark woods that she feared tripping over something and breaking a bone, yet she could still see the back of the house. It was such a strange delineation between light and darkness. Even with the encroaching storm, there was plenty of gray light to see by in the backyard. Panic fluttered softly against her rib cage and she turned in a circle.

"Please come talk to me," she said to the trees. "I promise I've only come to help."

Thunder grumbled off the horizon and the leaves above rustled in the wind. She didn't want to be caught in these trees when the rain started. She would never make her way back then.

"I know you're here. I saw you."

Something cold fluttered along her arms and she turned quickly to find the source. A pale silver orb floated a few feet away.

"Hello," she said. "I've come to help you."

The orb bounced a little making a wavy line of light in the air. It circled her before breaking into a dozen smaller orbs. She could feel them—the anguish of their souls and their disbelief in her ability to help them.

"I truly am here to help," she whispered. "But you must talk to me first. How did you come to be here?"

The voices hummed through her head—each one wanting desperately to share their story—but their voices mingled too much for her to single them out. The sound grew louder and louder in her head until she could not hear anything outside of herself. Charlie squeezed her eyes shut and pressed her hands to her ears.

"Stop, please, I can only hear you one at a time."

The voices stopped completely. When she opened her eyes, a single girl stood before her. The girl wore a tattered brown skirt and a sweat-stained linen blouse, just like in her dream. Ruth Mathis.

"I know you. I dreamed about you. You're Ruth."

The girl nodded.

"Ruth, do you see a light?"

The girl glanced around before her gaze settled on Charlie again. She shook her head. Charlie pursed her lips. It was a long shot to hope it would be as simple as telling the girl not to fear the light, but instead just to walk toward it.

"Ruth, do you know where he put you?"

Ruth's dark eyes widened, and she nodded slowly.

"Can you show me? Maybe if I find the place, then maybe it will free you."

Without warning, Ruth turned and ran deeper into the woods. Her apparition reduced to a single point of light—a silvery orb—and Charlie took a deep breath and followed her.

* * *

HER FLASHLIGHT DIED FIVE MINUTES INTO HER QUEST. IT dimmed to faint yellow before the light completely disappeared. She shook the dead cylinder, but when it did not come back to life, she shoved it back inside her bag and pulled out her cell phone. She pressed the center button, but the phone was dead too.

"Dammit," she whispered.

The heavy grayness of the woods pressed in on her and she could no longer see the house. The organic stink of the marsh wafted thick through the trees but at least the brush had thinned. She didn't have to fear tripping and falling, or worse, knocking herself unconscious. Her eyes searched for the silver orb and caught sight of it just as it disappeared behind a tree.

"Ruth," Charlie called into the milky gloom. "I can't see very well. Please come back."

She held her breath and waited. No response. Charlie reached inside her bag and wrapped her hand around one of the cool stones. She took a deep breath and headed for the place she last saw the pale, floating sphere.

Movement ahead of her made her heart jump into her throat. Blood hammered through her ears and instinctively she hunkered down behind one of the thick tree trunks. Slowly she peeked around the base of the tree concealing her. A man walked through the woods. She had dreamed of him enough to recognize his shape. He had come from the other side of the woods and carried a shovel against his shoulder.

Charlie took a deep breath and raised herself into a half-crouch. She kept her eyes on his dark form as it moved among the trees but wished she could see better.

The sound of a girl whimpering filled her head and tiny pinpricks of light appeared among the low brush and bases of trees. The pale spheres grew larger, casting just enough light for her to see her way forward. Charlie followed the bouncing lights.

He stopped near the edge of the woods. Through the trees, she could see the darkening marsh in the distance. Thunder clapped, closer now, but it didn't seem to bother him. The orbs flitted upwards and Charlie's gaze shifted, following them. Through the canopy of leaves, she could still see some sky. Grey and black clouds sailed by at a fast pace. The storm would be on top of them soon. Panic wound around her heart and squeezed. She wanted to stay and see what he was up to, but she also didn't want to get caught beneath the trees once lightning joined the party. Maybe she should just head back to her car. Give Jason a call. Tell him what she'd seen. Surely, he'd bring reinforcements, especially since they were looking for this man.

She glanced back at the trees where she'd last seen him. He was gone. Her breath stuttered in her chest and she quickly scanned the trees looking for any sign of him. Where had he gone? She moved closer to where he'd stopped.

A spray of dirt hit the mound not far from her, and she froze, holding her breath. The sound of metal cutting through earth came from somewhere in front of the growing mound of soil. Where was he? More dirt sprayed over the top of the heap, hitting the leaf litter on the other side. Charlie took cautious steps backwards, making as little noise as she could until she reached a nearby tree. She watched the pile grow, little by little, and her gut twisted tighter with each sound of the shovel scraping through dirt. She would hide until he finished whatever he was doing, then she would hightail it back to the house. Call Jason. Call Lisa and Jen. Do whatever it took to stop him. If she couldn't stop Talmadge, she would make sure his lackey didn't get away with his plans of adding to his collection.

Her thighs began to ache from crouching and she leaned against the rough bark of the tree. Cold air swirled around her neck and the air pressure changed. Thunder cracked overhead and the sounds of fat drops of rain drumming against the leaves echoed through the trees. Wet drops landed on her skin, driving her to her feet. She would come back with reinforcements.

His hand wrapped around her neck and he slammed her against the tree, knocking the breath out of her. She flailed her arms and tried to call out, but the only noise she could make was grunting. His grip tightened and her hands went to scratch him, but they swiped right through his barely visible arms. He locked his gaze on hers and smiled.

"I told you I would break you," Aldus Talmadge said.

The edges of her vision grew dark, and she stared into his inky, unforgiving eyes just before the world went black.

CHAPTER 28

"**S**top the car!" Jen said from the seat next to him. The urgency in her voice made him hit the brakes.

"What? What is it?"

"Graveyard." Jen looked at him as if she'd just explained what she meant in detail.

"Okay. So?"

"Just pull in. I need to get something."

Jason threw a glance over his shoulder to Lisa. "Is she for real? We're almost there."

Lisa shrugged and nodded. "She's for real."

Jason's lips twisted into a scowl and he put the car in reverse. He pulled into the parking lot of the Talmadge Island Presbyterian Church. No lights were on inside and the building looked empty. The hair on his arms stood up, but he ignored it.

"Pull around behind the building," Jen ordered. "There's a cemetery back there, I'm sure of it."

Jason did as he was told and parked close to the open metal gate of the old cemetery. A white Chevy truck was backed into the corner space and Jason eyed it. Maybe it belonged to a caretaker. He wrestled with the urge to check the license plate.

"I'll be right back." Jen hopped from the car before he could respond. He watched her disappear into the shadows. Shiny obelisks and large granite stones marked newer graves near the front of the large, shady plot of land. Toward the back, deep in the gloom, he could see simpler tall, flat headstones and several crypts. The whole place made his skin crawl.

"Should we go with her?" Jason asked.

"Nope, she's fine. She's just getting some graveyard dirt."

"Okay." He turned in his seat and glared at the two women in his backseat. "What is she gonna do with that?"

Daphne looked up from her phone, her expression uncertain. Lisa shrugged and her lips curved as if she had a secret she didn't want to share.

"What?" Jason's voice rose sharply.

Daphne quirked one eyebrow. "Well, if you must

know, Jen will probably use it to help Charlie get rid of this nasty ancestor of yours."

"I kinda hope it doesn't come to that." Lisa stared at the graveyard through the window. "It's dangerous to summon a reaper."

"What are you talking about?" Jason understood the words they said, but it was still like they were speaking some secret language. His gaze bounced from Lisa to Daphne and he frowned. Maybe Charlie wasn't the only crazy person in her family.

"Should we tell him?" Daphne's delicate features shifted to amusement.

"No," Lisa said, her expression opaque. "He's not ready." Her hazel eyes studied him as if she were seeing into the heart of him. He fought the urge to squirm like a little boy under her scrutiny. "He barely believes as it is."

Daphne tilted her pixie face. "You're right."

Lisa's attention shifted from him to the front window. "Jen's taking too long."

"Maybe she didn't have a gift?" Daphne offered.

Lisa shook her head, resting her hand on the door handle. "No, that's not it. Come on."

"I thought you said she'd be fine." Jason glanced into the thickening shadows. Thunder boomed overhead, and he leaned forward to look at the black cloud moving overhead.

"Well, I can be wrong." Lisa pulled the handle and pushed against the door.

"Ha!" Daphne snorted. "You'd better record that, Jason. Lisa never admits to being wrong." She opened her door, too, and jumped out to join her cousin.

"Great. That's just great," Jason muttered to himself. He climbed out of his car. "It's gonna rain!"

Neither woman acknowledged him and he kicked his toe against the front tire. He sighed and followed them into the cemetery.

RAY KURTZ STOPPED IN HIS TRACKS WHEN HE SAW THE pretty, young woman dash across the cemetery. He slid silently into the deep shadow of a large tree and watched her go from grave to grave as if she were looking for something. *Or somebody*, he thought. He tapped his fingers against the bark.

"Come on," he whispered. He had things to do. If she didn't leave soon, he would just take her and throw her into the pit with the others. What was one more girl?

Finally, she stopped in front of one of the older stones. He could hear her talking aloud to it, but from this distance couldn't quite make out what she was saying. She had a bag slung across her body and she reached inside and pulled something out, placing it on top of the headstone.

"Jen?" a woman's voice called.

"Over here," the pretty woman answered. When she stood, it looked like she had scooped up some soil from the grave. She shoved it into her bag and turned to meet a pretty blonde and another brunette. A moment later, a man joined them. He recognized the cop. A lump formed in his throat—an icy pebble threatening to choke him. What if the cop decided to check out his truck?

The rain began to fall, slow and sparse at first. The sky opened up and began to pour. The brunette with the chin-length hair shrieked and covered her hair with her hands. They all ran toward the parking lot. He moved closer to the fence, but stuck to the shadows. All four of them climbed into a black muscle car and sped off.

Only when he was sure they were no longer in the church parking lot did he allow himself to go to his truck to get the other girl and the duct tape.

CHAPTER 29

The Uber driver pulled into the circular drive in front of Talmadge House and stopped in front of the wide porch steps.

"You sure this is where you want to go?" the woman asked. Sugar had learned her name was Lorraine, and she was driving for Uber for a little extra money to pay for her daughter's music lessons. Her daughter had been accepted by a prestigious teacher, but the lessons were expensive. Sugar listened to her, nodding where appropriate and making all the polite conversation she could stand.

"Oh, yes, thank you." Sugar finished the transaction on her phone.

"It looks sort of haunted," Lorraine said. "Not that I believe in that sort of thing."

"It is, dear." Sugar pulled a five-dollar bill from her wallet and handed it to Lorraine. "And it's all right if you don't believe. I wish I didn't."

Sugar rushed out of the car and up the steps before Lorraine could respond. The rain poured down on her in a sheet, soaking her to the skin. Once under the cover of the porch, she shook the water from her short, silver hair. She took a deep breath and walked to the front door. She knew Susan was out of town. How she was going to get in the house she didn't know, but something inside her told her she didn't need a key. She placed her hand on the knob, turned it and pushed. It didn't budge. A cold thread of panic wrapped around her heart. She licked her lips.

"Honey? I need you open the door for me."

Thunder cracked overhead, drowning out the sound of the deadbolt retracting, but Sugar felt the vibration of it. The door pulled inward on its own, creaking. Her heartbeat quickened and her stomach flopped over like a cold fish. She looked over her shoulder, but Lorraine and her cute little Prius were gone. What had she been thinking coming out here all alone? She hadn't told anyone anything other than she was going to her daughter's house. So stupid. Lightning flashed, illuminating the foyer and Honey appeared, beckoning her inside.

"Hurry, Sugar. Hurry. She needs you," Honey's ragged whisper wrapped around her senses, and the pebbling on her already chilled arms nearly doubled in size. Sugar stepped into the foyer and her sister floated over to the staircase. Honey raised her arm, motioning for her sister to follow. She'd already come this far. Sugar pulled the small gold cross hanging on the chain around her neck to her lips. The hallway light flipped on.

Pleas,e God, please don't let me die tonight. And if I do, please don't let my soul be trapped in this house. Amen.

Sugar put her hand on the old oak railing and started up the steps.

"OH, MY LORD. POOR BUTCH," SUGAR MUTTERED. SHE covered her mouth and glanced around. The sheer volume of junk accumulated on the landing and hallway overwhelmed her—stacks of newspapers, boxes, old toys, dishes, and books. How had things gotten this bad? Her heart ached with sadness for her older brother and guilt for not visiting when he was alive. Maybe if she'd seen this, maybe she could have done something to help him.

Honey drifted into their parent's old bedroom and the light came on. Sugar had to turn sideways to get past a stack of boxes and when she finally made her way inside their room, her breath caught in her throat. The room looked almost exactly the same as Sugar remembered it. The bed was still made with a faded patchwork quilt. Two side tables, each holding brass oil lamps with matching painted glass shades. Her father had converted them to electric not long after the war ended in 1945. On her mother's table was a small prayer book. It had never been this dirty when her mother lived, though, of that she was sure.

A thick layer of dust coated everything, and the fabrics had faded badly and were stained and shredding in places. Sugar cried out as a big fat palmetto bug skittered up the wall behind the spindle headboard. They were nothing more than flying roaches, and, oh, how she hated them. She used to make her brother Butch kill them because she couldn't stand the thought of one flying at her and getting caught in her hair. She shivered, and a shadow passed in front of the old-fashioned vanity, drawing her toward it. Her mother's silver-handled mirror and brush set were still in their tray. She traced a finger through the dust on top of the reflective glass. The shadow had not been anything otherworldly at all—just her father's strap, hanging from a nail on the wall beside the large vanity mirror. When it had made its way upstairs from the kitchen, she couldn't remember. She had feared that thick piece of leather so much as a child. It took on a life of its own in her father's hands, administering discipline and his idea of justice.

Take it, Sugar, Honey's soft whisper laced through her head. *Take it with you.*

"Why?" Sugar asked the empty room. Honey didn't answer directly. Instead, the nail bent down and the strap spilled onto the floor. Sugar sighed and picked it up. The strap felt heavy in her hand. "What am I supposed to do with this?"

The bedroom light went out, submerging Sugar in darkness. The hallway light flickered, and downstairs, Sugar heard a door banging.

Sugar made her way downstairs again. The front door was still closed, so she wove her way through the stacks of junk to the kitchen. Wind hissed through the rusty screen door and the back door swung in the wind, slamming into the kitchen wall. She got hold of the door and started to close it, but the sight of them made her stop. A half-dozen silvery orbs floated at the edge of the woods. Sugar's body went cold, and she took a step back.

She's with them. Help her.

THE FRONT DOOR WAS LOCKED UP TIGHT WHEN JASON arrived. He used the key his mother had given him, letting the three women into the house. He flipped the light switch near the front door and the foyer light flickered before coming on.

"Charlie!" Jen called up the steps.

"I doubt she's in the house," Jason said. "The door was locked.

"Uh-huh." Jen nodded, but her tone was dismissive. "Charlie!"

Jason looked to Lisa, using his hands to gesture his disbelief. Lisa frowned. "Jen, I don't think she's here."

A gust of wind swept through the hallway and some loose papers and damp leaves swirled into the foyer.

"What the—?" Jason started.

Daphne peered through the double doors leading to the hallway running beneath the grand staircase. "I think it's coming from through there."

Jason moved toward the kitchen and the three women trailed after him. The back door was wide open causing a tunnel effect. Jason scanned the kitchen, the hair on the back of his neck and arms standing alert. Lisa took hold of the door, stopping it before it banged into the wall. The rain had slowed down, but the storm was far from over. Thunder cracked in the distance, followed closely by a wide streak of lightning.

"Jason, is that your grandma?" Lisa pointed at the screen door. Daphne and Jen crowded behind her. The old woman ambled slowly toward the edge of the woods, taking care not to slip on the slick, wet grass.

"What?" Jason pushed in front of them. "Oh, my God. Gran." His heart sped up at the sight of her and he was out the door and halfway across the yard before he remembered the women. He threw a quick look over this shoulder and found them trailing close behind. Jen jogged in front of the other two with her hand shoved into her bag.

"Gran!" he called. His grandmother reached the edge of the trees before he could shout her name again. The rain fell steady, and he kept having to wipe the cold water from his eyes. He blinked, not sure what he was seeing. Jason slowed for a moment and Jen caught up to him.

"Do you see that?" he asked. Several pale silver lights bounced among the trees, advancing deeper into the woods.

"Yes," Jen said, speaking loudly over the sounds of the storm. "They look like they could be ghost lights."

"I don't like this. Not one bit," he muttered. A cold lump blocked his throat and his heart beat faster.

"Come on," she said. "Let's see what they want."

They started into the woods again, moving as fast as they could, despite the rain. Once he caught up to his grandmother, they were going to have a long chat about storms and following strange lights.

CHAPTER 30

Sugar froze when she spied the man's silhouette in the darkness. Even in the dim gloom of the rain and twilight she knew the motion he made with the tool in his hands. Her heart hammered against the sides of her chest and her whole body went cold. If it weren't for the ghostly lights, she would have moved slower through the underbrush.

She heard Jason call "Gran!" his voice caught between the sound of the rain and the wind. He was a determined boy, though. She knew he'd catch up with her soon.

She made her way through the bushes and saplings, watching as the man dug in to the mound of dirt with a shovel.

"I don't think I can do this, Honey," she murmured. An icy hand pressed against her back between her shoulder blades, holding her steady. It gave her a gentle push forward.

This is how I died.

Honey's words scratched across Sugar's heart. The pale lights flew away from her, heading toward him. Her fingers tightened around the leather in her hand. This was how her sister died. There was nothing she could do to save Honey. Nothing she could do about the fear and guilt that she had run from for so many years. But she could do something here and now. Rage ignited deep inside her belly. That was someone's daughter, someone's sister, someone's niece that he buried. It had to stop. She had to stop him. Sugar raised her hand, charging forward, her old body complying without complaint. She opened her mouth and began to screech.

* * *

SOMETHING PELTED HER FACE, ROUSING HER. HER HAND searched for the culprit and she pinched bits of mud and sand and tiny stones between her fingertips. Charlie opened her eyes and breathed in the sweet scent of rain and wet soil. Her shoulder ached from lying on her side and she felt something warm against her back but when she tried to move, her legs wouldn't comply. She turned her head and saw the shadow of him standing above her, shovel in hand. Her breath came in quick bursts, but only through her nose. Panic threatened to choke her as realization bloomed. Her hands and feet were bound by duct tape. Another shovelful of dirt rained down on her, and she instinctively raised her hands in front of her face. She tried to scream, but the sound competed with the thunder and the blood barreling through her ears.

Think, Charlie. Think.

It wouldn't take long for him to cover her with enough soil to make it impossible to move. A soft groan came from behind her and the girl on the television screen flashed through her mind. Charlie felt the warmth against her body. There were two of them in this grave. This was how Aldus Talmadge was adding to his collection.

Charlie swallowed back the bile gathering in her throat. She had already lived through this once in a dream. She squeezed her eyes shut. She had wanted to die so badly two years ago, wanted all the pain in this world to just end. But now, there was too much to live for —her son, her family. More than anything, she wanted to hug her uncle Jack's neck and hang out on Friday nights with her cousins. And how would she ever get to know Jason? Another shovel full of dirt struck her, hitting her hip this time. Hot tears burned a trail from the corners of her eyes. This was not the way her life was supposed to end. She struggled against the duct tape wrapped around her wrists, wriggling it back and forth. If she could get her hands free, maybe she could escape this place.

Where had Ruth gotten to? Was Talmadge keeping her away? Or maybe he had used her to lure her in further. A cold pang yawned inside her chest, threatening to swallow her whole. If he buried her in this hole—no one would know. She would just become one more trinket in Talmadge's collection. Under his thumb for eternity.

Her hand slipped, the tape loosened just a little, and her knuckle banged against something soft and hard at the same time. Her fingers hunted for the source. Her bag. He hadn't removed her bag. After fumbling with the flap, she pushed her bound hands inside, searching for the bone handled knife. Something smooth and cold brushed against the back of her hand. The stones. Another stab of panic pricked her heart. Jen's words floated through her head. *Once you've picked a stone, call on a spirit guide to help you.*

Charlie wrapped her hand around the stone. Breathing in and out through her nose as best she could, she shut out the world around her and the ache in her chest. Would this even work? Did she believe? If she wanted to live, she had to at least try, didn't she? Yes. Because more than anything, she wanted to live.

Spirit guide, I don't know if you can hear me. I don't know if you really exist. If you do, please help me. Please, help me live.

Charlie waited—for what, she wasn't sure. An inner voice? An apparition? The silence inside her spread, inky and dark. Tears burned at the back of her throat and the corners of her eyes. She sniffled and moved her hand around the bag, searching for the knife. It looked like she was on her own after all. Finally, her fingers found the ridges of the bone-handled blade. She maneuvered it open and struggled to move it to the right place. Her sweat and the rain had let her stretch it just enough though, and the sharp edge found purchase against the sticky edge of the tape. She pushed her wrists away from each other, making the tape taut. The blade slid through the thick layers of plastic but only a little at a time. Another shovel full of dirt hit her legs.

Somewhere above her head, light swirled, drawing her attention. She shifted her head. Silvery orbs spun so fast around the man, the light trailed after them, creating a near perfect circle. He stopped digging into the pile and struck at them with his shovel. The orbs swooped closer to his head, the terror on his face was visible only for a brief second in the light, but when the banshee-like scream came from somewhere behind him, he turned his back to her and held his shovel up, ready to strike at whatever was headed his way.

CHAPTER 31

"Break your binding," a young woman's voice said. Ruth Mathis appeared, hovering over her legs and a chill settled over her feet.

"How?" Charlie asked.

"Break your binding," Ruth repeated.

Break your binding. The words hummed through her head. She had heard something similar before. But where? Then, she remembered. Brian and his escape tricks.

Charlie kicked her legs free of as much dirt as she could and scooted onto her back. What had Brian done? She closed her eyes and tried to recall how he'd swung his arms. She'd been so distracted that day.

Pushing against the young woman lying beside her, she raised her arms above her head and tightened her core. With a swift downward motion, her hands hit her belly and the duct tape gave way, but didn't tear completely. She brought her wrists to her mouth. Her teeth ripped through the piece still holding her wrists together and she spit the sticky tape to the side. Her hands were free. She sat up and used the knife to cut through the tape around her feet.

Charlie turned to the girl and brushed her wet hair away from her face. "It's going to be all right. I'm gonna get us out of here."

The girl groaned, and her eyes fluttered open for a second and closed again.

Charlie pushed to her feet and found the hole was only about three feet deep. The orbs still distracted the man, enabling her to pull herself out on the opposite side of the hole.

When she got to her feet, she readied herself to run, but the motion of the man ducking and shouting at his attacker stopped her. It took a moment to process what she was seeing—Sugar Blackburn was beating the man with what looked like a wide belt. He tried to strike back at her, but the silver orbs kept flying at his face.

Quietly, Charlie slunk around the hole. If she could get him around the waist from behind, and grab hold of the shovel's handle, maybe she could bring him down. She took several breaths and blew out hard on the last one then charged forward.

Her shoulder connected with his lower back, and she knocked her fist into the back of his knee, narrowly missing the swing of the long shovel handle. She felt his body buckle, and the ground rose to meet them. He tried to push himself up, but Charlie climbed up his body and put her knee in his back. She shoved his head down and straddled him.

"Sugar! Get the shovel out of his hand." Sugar stared at her for a second, dumbfounded. The man bucked his body, almost throwing her off. "Sugar! Please! Help me."

Sugar moved into action, striking the hand gripping the shovel hard with the strap. He had some sort of brace wrapped around his forearm and he screamed. She yanked the shovel away from him and threw it out of his reach.

"Gran!" A man's voice startled both women.

The man beneath Charlie threw her off his back and she landed hard on her side. He pushed up into a runner's stance and started to bolt. Charlie grabbed him by his nearest leg in a hammerlock with her ankles, and twisted. He fell flat onto his face.

Jason moved in fast, twisting the man's arm behind him. He pushed the man down by his neck and knelt, shoving his knee into his back.

"Charlie, can you get the cuffs hanging from the back of my belt?" Jason asked, sounding calmer than she expected.

Charlie quickly did as he asked. Jason snapped the cuffs tightly around the man's wrists.

"Jason, the girl is here," Charlie said. "She's still alive, but she's unconscious."

Jason nodded, pulled his cell phone from his pocket, and made a call.

"We'll have officers here shortly," he said. "Are you all right?"

Charlie nodded. "Yes."

"I'm going back to the house to wait for my team to show up. Can you stay here with her?"

"Of course," Charlie said.

"I'm staying too," Sugar said dully.

"You sure, Gran?"

"Yes."

"All right. I'll be back soon."

They watched as Jason trudged through the woods with the handcuffed man in tow. Charlie moved in close to Sugar. "You sure you're all right?"

Sugar's eyes darted around the woods. The rain had reduced to barely a mist, but fat drops still fell from the leaves. Her hand dangled by her side, still gripping the strap tightly.

"Yes." Sugar sounded uneasy. She gave the three young women standing nearby a sideways glance. "Where did they go?"

Charlie knew exactly who she meant, and she glanced

around, looking for the ghostly lights that had led her to
this place, but they were gone. Had they moved on? The
dread coiling in Charlie's stomach told her no. They were
still here. Still trapped beneath Aldus Talmadge's thumb.
She touched the old woman's upper arm. Jen, Lisa, and
Daphne drew in around them, and Jen put her hand on
the center of Charlie's back.

"I don't know," Charlie whispered.

The first orb appeared to Charlie's left, glowing pale
and white. It morphed into the shape of a young woman.
One by one, the orbs formed a circle around them,
becoming apparitions of the young women they once
were. Charlie recognized Ruth and Honey and a fresh
pang filled her chest when Daniela, the missing girl she
dreamed of appeared.

The air stilled, and a chill settled around them.
Without warning, Lisa screamed and was yanked
backwards. Her hands went to her throat, and she gasped
and wheezed, trying to catch her breath.

"Show yourself, you coward," Charlie spat out the
words.

Aldus Talmadge appeared behind Lisa, his arm
around her neck in a chokehold. She clawed at his arm,
but her hands went through him.

"Let her go," Charlie snapped.

"You think you bested me," he said, his black eyes

narrowing. "But you haven't. You have taken something I love, and so now I will take something you love."

"You do that, and I will hunt you for eternity."

"You don't have eternity," he said.

Charlie pulled the sharp knife from her pocket and unfolded the blade. She pressed it to the skin of her wrist.

Jen stepped up beside her and put her hand over Charlie's. "No. You are not allowed to do this. There's another way."

Jen bent down and dug through the top layer of wet leaves until she found a wide, dry one underneath. She reached inside her bag and retrieved a tiny bit of wet soil.

"Mrs. Blackburn, I need a drop of your blood," Jen said softly.

Sugar looked from Charlie to Jen and then to the apparition of her ancestor holding Lisa captive. Sugar nodded and held out her hand.

Jen gently slipped the knife out of Charlie's hand and poked the sharp tip into Sugar's finger. She squeezed the digit tight, letting blood drop into the soil on top of the leaf.

"Are you sure about this?" Charlie asked.

Jen nodded and turned Charlie's hand palm up. She placed the leaf in the center. She reached inside her bag one more time and pulled out a small baggy of white powder and a lighter.

"Jen, you should be doing this. I don't have—"

"You're the one he's attached to. You're the one who has to stop him. Don't be scared. It won't burn you, I promise." Jen took a large pinch of powder and sprinkled it over the soil and blood, while muttering an incantation. Charlie sniffed and the soft baby scent tickled her nose. Talcum powder. Charlie's heart beat faster. With a flick of Jen's lighter, the powder caught fire and flared. Charlie stepped forward with the fireball in her hand and Jen continued the incantation until the inky shadow morphed from the darkness. It loomed up behind Talmadge, morphing into the shape of black robes. The blade of its scythe glimmered with an inner light.

A slow hiss echoed around them. Jen turned her head away and grabbed hold of Sugar's hand. "Look away, Mrs. Blackburn."

Charlie stepped up to Talmadge and looked him in the eye. "You are no longer bound to this land. You have no more power here. It's time for you to move on."

Talmadge began to laugh.

The fireball had consumed the leaf, dirt, and blood, and Charlie took the ash in her hand and moved it to Talmadge's forehead, letting it fall through him.

He opened his mouth to speak but choked on the words. His arm dropped from around Lisa's neck and she fell forward, landing hard on her hands and knees. She gasped and coughed. Talmadge's gaze trailed down his body. The sharp end of the curved blade protruded from his chest. He let out a sharp, loud keening as the reaper collected him. The sound made Charlie's bones ache. She'd only seen the reaper twice—each time acting as harbinger. Instinctively, she squeezed her eyes shut, and when she opened them, Talmadge and the reaper were gone. One by one, the spirits of the girls ascended toward an opening in the canopy, their light twirling until they faded into mist.

CHAPTER 32

"Oh, my God, I can't believe this, the views keep coming." Daphne slid into the booth next to Charlie with her phone in her hand. "Over 14,000 views and I haven't even really promoted it beyond a couple of tweets and a post in an occult group on Facebook."

"I can't believe you were recording video the whole time." Charlie held her nose over her coffee cup and breathed in the heavenly scent of chocolate, cream and coffee before taking a sip.

Daphne grinned. "That was the whole reason we got involved in the first place."

"Yeah, well, I still don't think it's a good idea to show it." Jen sipped her coffee.

"Oh, what's the harm?" Daphne scoffed. She cut her

short stack with the side of her fork and stabbed the bite of her three pancakes. "It's not like there's anything more than a bunch of silver lights and a dark shadow and, of course, Charlie's pyrotechnics."

Charlie nibbled on her last piece of bacon. "You mean Jen's pyrotechnics."

"Whatever. It looks fantastic."

"Well, I agree with Jen—I don't know how smart it is to court—" Lisa leaned in close to the table and whispered the finish, "a reaper."

"Y'all are paranoid. You can barely see him." Daphne took a bite of pancake.

"Speaking of courting," Lisa said, directing her gaze toward Charlie. "How's your boyfriend?"

"How many times do I have to tell you? He. Is not. My boyfriend," Charlie protested.

"Uh-huh." Lisa nodded. "So, are you helping him?"

"Not much left to do, really. Ray Kurtz broke down, admitted to everything, taking the girls, raping and killing the first girl and burying her in the woods. He even admitted to breaking into my apartment and attacking me. Of course, he also said he did it because the voices told him to, so who knows exactly where he'll end up."

"Well, I, for one, am glad you're moving out of there." Jen stretched her arm across the table and touched Charlie's arm.

"Me too." Charlie smiled and took another sip of her coffee.

"You know, with all these views, people are going to want more." Daphne grinned.

"Daphne, just back off," Lisa warned.

"It's okay. I've already decided to give readings more regularly for clients. Help them and their loved ones connect one last time. If a troublesome spirit comes up, at least I know I can help."

"And you've got us to back you up," Jen offered.

"Thank God for that," Charlie said.

"What about Jason? Is he going to be one of your clients now?"

Charlie quirked an eyebrow. "We're taking it on a case-by-case basis. There may even be some consulting fees involved."

Lisa's hazel eyes shined, and she gave Charlie an approving grin. "Nice. Keep your receipts. Business expenses."

"Yes, ma'am." Charlie glanced at the clock hanging behind the counter at The Kitchen Witch Cafe. She slung the strap of her bag across her body and pushed gently against Daphne. "In the meantime, I've got to get to work. There's a co-worker there who really needs my help."

CHARLIE WALKED INTO THE WOMEN'S BATHROOM AND checked every stall to make sure she was alone. Then she turned the lock on the door.

"Helen?" Charlie asked. "I know you're here."

"Well, of course, I'm here," Helen snapped, her voice coming from behind Charlie. "Where else am I going to be?"

Slowly, Charlie turned and faced her deceased coworker. "You know, I can't believe I've never thought about this before. But what exactly is it that you're waiting for?"

"What am I waiting for?"

"Yes. I've been seeing spirits since I was five and the ones that get stuck, like you, are almost always waiting for something. I really don't think you were damned to stay here for all eternity. In fact, I'm gonna crawl out on a limb, and say I know you're not. But if I'm gonna help you, I need to know what you're waiting for."

Helen's bottom lip quivered. "I guess I'm just waiting for that scrawny little supervisor to get a taste of his own medicine."

"What medicine is that? You told me you can't leave this bathroom. That you would haunt him if you could. But I don't believe you really want to do that. I believe what you really want is just to move on, but something inside your head—"

"What head? I don't have a head anymore."

"Yes, you do. Just like you still have a heart. What do you want him to know, Helen?"

Helen paused and her dark eyes shimmered with wetness. Could a ghost cry? Or was it just a manifestation of some remembered emotion? The apparition's chest heaved and released an audible sigh.

"I want him to know that I understand about rules and policies. But I also want him to understand that he's dealing with human beings, not machines, and sometimes it's more important to be compassionate and to try to understand what your employees are going through."

A chill settled around Charlie's heart. "What were you going through, Helen?"

Helen placed her hand just above her left breast. "It was my heart you see—" Her fingers tapped against her gossamer chest. "It was failing me. The doctors had me on all sorts of medicine. They wanted me to quit my job, stay home, and die. But I just couldn't. I wasn't ready. But some days when I woke up, it was hard to breathe, and I just needed a little extra rest. At the same time, I had to come to work. I needed the health insurance to help me pay for the medicine. That's all. I just wanted him to look at me like I was a human being, and ask me what was going on. Instead, he looked at me like I was just another chronic rule breaker he had to deal with. You know I worked for this company for twenty-two years."

"That's a really long time."

"Yes, it is. Too long for them to just write me off."

"I'm so sorry, Helen. You know what I think?"

"What?"

"I think we should write him a letter. I think we should write him a letter and tell him everything that you just told me. I can't promise you it will change anything. In fact, I'm pretty sure it won't. But maybe it will free you, which is way more important."

"And you would help me with that?"

"Absolutely." Charlie said. "I would be happy to. In fact, I can't wait to hand him the letter and say this is from Helen Jackson."

Helen smiled wide for a moment but it faded as quickly as it came. "What if it doesn't work? What if I really am damned to stay here for all eternity?"

"Well, first of all, I think it will work. And second of all, if it doesn't, then I think you need to make up your mind to leave this bathroom and go haunt his scrawny ass for the rest of his tenure at this company."

Helen laughed, and it was the best sound Charlie had heard all day. "I think that is a brilliant idea."

"Just remember it's Plan B. Plan A is to get you where you're supposed to be, which is clearly not here."

"Alright-y then. Let's get started."

Charlie pulled a pen and notebook out of her bag. "Great." She smiled. "Just tell me what you want it to say."

* * *

CHARLIE CAREFULLY FOLDED THE LETTER INTO THIRDS AND slid it into the envelope. "It's done."

"Yeah," Helen said.

"Do you feel any differently? Is there a white light?"

"No, not yet," Helen said. "There is one thing I've seen. I'm just not sure exactly what it is."

"You want to talk about it?"

"Maybe I should show you instead." Helen drifted to the first stall and moved through the door.

"You know I can't do that, right?"

"Of course. I'm dead, not stupid," Helen quipped.

Some part of Charlie was going to miss Helen. "Come in here."

Charlie sighed and pushed open the door. Helen's head and torso hovered over the toilet and her legs disappeared into the bowl. The sight sent a shiver crawling over Charlie shoulders. There were just some things she would never get used to.

"Okay. What is it that you want to show me?"

"Take a look at that hook on the back of the door." Helen said. "Look closely."

Charlie turned around and leaned in close, looking at the white plastic hook large enough to hold a coat and a purse. In the center of the white plate where the hook attached was a tiny black opening. She squinted at it, unsure exactly what she was seeing.

"Helen? What am I looking at?"

"I don't know exactly. When I first woke up in here, it made a little buzzing noise. Till I touched it. It hasn't buzzed again since."

"Okay?"

"All I know is that every single stall has one," Helen said. "And it gives me a bad feeling."

"Okay," Charlie said, still not sure exactly what she was looking at. "You've shown me. Now, what about that light?"

Helen smiled wide, her teeth gleaming. "Oh, yes. I see it now. Thank you, Charlie. Thank you so much."

Charlie watched as Helen faded and for the first time in her life she knew exactly why she was made the way she was, why she saw what she saw, and heard what she heard, and she wasn't afraid.

CHAPTER 33

Charlie took a deep breath and raised her hand to knock on Dylan's door. He was the only supervisor who constantly kept his door shut. She didn't even want to hazard a guess at what he did in there. A soft moan came from the other side of the door. Maybe she didn't have to. She tucked the envelope into the back pocket of her jeans, placed her hand on the knob and, as quietly as she could, pushed the door open. All the supervisors had two desks in their office and the faux wood monstrosities were configured into an L-shape with one desk against a side wall and one desk between the supervisor and the door. Two chairs faced the supervisor's desk for meeting with their reps or other visitors.

Dylan had his tall faux-leather chair turned away

from the door, facing the two computer monitors on the desk facing the wall. Charlie could easily see the monitor with the call center software up on the screen showing who was on calls, who was on break, who was in a wrap-up code and how long. The other monitor had been turned, so it was not quite so easy to see.

She moved a little closer and craned her neck until she could see the other monitor better. It looked like some sort of video of several bathroom stalls. One of them was occupied by her co-worker, Sara Milner. She edged closer to his desk, and it took a moment for her brain to register exactly what she was seeing. Dylan, with his pants unzipped and his hand stuck inside his boxer shorts.

"Oh, my God," she muttered. Her hand flew to her mouth, and she backed away. "Oh, my God."

Dylan's half-closed eyes flew open and for a moment he struggled to get his hand out of his pants and to stand up.

"What are you doing in here?" he snapped, fumbling with his belt and zipper.

"I think a better question is what are *you* doing in here?" Cameras. That's what Helen had shown her. Charlie paced, fuming. "I cannot believe you! You are just a disgusting little troll."

"Hey—you should be careful. You're not exactly the

most stable of my employees, and I have video to prove it. You talking to yourself in the bathroom."

"Seriously? Have you lost your freaking mind?" She raised her voice. Hopefully, it would get the attention of one of the other supervisors or better yet the call center manager. She didn't want to leave him here alone in case he could somehow destroy his evidence. "I catch you in here masturbating to women going to the bathroom. So, you're the one that planted the cameras!"

"Is there a problem in here?" The call center manager Joan Ridley poked her head in. She wore black pants, a red silk top, and every piece of her salt and pepper hair was perfectly in place. "Dylan, are you all right?"

"I think a better question, Joan, would be, are your workers all right? I just caught Dylan with his hands in his pants masturbating to images of women using the bathroom."

"Charlie, those are some very serious allegations." Joan stepped inside the office and folded her arms across her chest.

"They are. And you better believe I'm going to go to HR about them, and maybe even the police, because clearly what he's done is plant cameras in there. Which has to be illegal?" She couldn't wait to ask Jason later.

"Dylan?" Joan asked. "What is she talking about?"

"Nothing—Joan, it's fine. I have this under control."

"What exactly do you have under control?" Joan frowned.

"Charlie. I'm afraid she's not exactly been our most stable worker. I've been trying to cover up for her and give her the benefit of the doubt but—"

"Oh, no, you don't get to do that. You don't get to make me sound like I'm crazy. Joan, I would like you to get someone from HR to accompany you and me to the bathroom, and I'd like to get someone from IT here to check his computer for a live feed to those cameras."

Joan stared at her for a moment, flustered before finally picking up the phone on Dylan's desk.

"Hey, Roger, it's Joan over in the call center. Do you have a moment to step into Dylan Henderson's office? Yes, it appears we have a situation here. I have a rep accusing one of my supervisors of lewd behavior. Sure. Thanks." Joan hung up the phone and walked over to the computer.

"Joan? Seriously, you don't believe her?" Dylan stepped in front of the monitor, a defensive ring in his voice.

"Honestly, Dylan, I don't know what to believe at this point. But Charlie's made a complaint, and I'm obligated to look into it. If you've done nothing wrong, then there isn't really anything to worry about, is there?"

Dylan's pale face blanched to an unnatural shade of

white. If he'd been see-through, Charlie would've assumed he was a ghost.

A few minutes later, Roger Hill entered the office along with two members of the IT department. Charlie recognized one of them as Micah Hodges. They had been in the same new hire orientation seven years ago. Micah sat down at Dylan's computer and his fingers whizzed across the keyboard.

"I'll be damned," Micah said. "There's definitely of feed of cameras coming to this computer. I'm really surprised we didn't pick up the signal before now."

Dylan crossed his arms. "I have no idea how that got on there."

Roger's gray bushy eyebrows furrowed. "Joan, Dylan. You need to come with me to my office."

"Of course," Joan said.

"Do you need me anymore?" Charlie asked. "I need to get back on the phone."

"Thank you, Charlie, we'll call you when we need you," Roger said, giving her a perfunctory smile.

"Oh, and, Dylan," Charlie said. "This is for you." She pulled the envelope with his name out of her pocket.

"What's this?" He stared down at it with a distasteful look on his face.

"It's a letter from Helen Jackson," Charlie said.

"Helen Jackson died, Charlie," Joan said.

"Yes, ma'am, she did. But she still had a few things she needed to say to Dylan."

She pressed the envelope into his hands. "Read it."

Charlie gave Dylan one last look of disgust.

Her whole body felt lighter as she walked away.

Maybe being true to herself wouldn't be so hard after all.

A NOTE FROM WENDY

Thank you for reading Haunting Charlie. If you've come this far then hopefully it's because you enjoyed getting to know Charlie and her cousins. Their spooky adventures continue in a series of spine-tingling, supernatural suspenses, full of chills, thrills and more of the characters you love.

In the next story, Wayward Spirits Charlie finds herself working with Deputy Tate on two cases - a cold case for a missing girl, and the mysterious death of a woman.

Both cases are full of buried secrets and spirits that just won't rest in peace. And Charlie will have to embrace her witch heritage to protect herself because a ghost with a grudge isn't just dangerous. It's deadly.

A GIFT FOR READER'S OF MY NEWSLETTER

If you sign up for my newsletter you'll get exclusive content, and announcements for preorders and new releases when they're launched. The first exclusive you get is a deleted scene from Haunting Charlie. Sign up

now and I'll send you the link to download it. http://
eepurl.com/czMPgi

CONNECT WITH ME

Want to comment on your favorite scene? Or make suggestions for a funny ghostly encounter for Charlie? Or tell me what sort of magic you'd like to see Jen, Daphne and Lisa perform? Like my Facebook page and let me know. I post content there regularly and talk with my readers every day.

Facebook: https://www.facebook.com/wendywangauthor

Let's talk about our favorite books in my readers group on Facebook.

Readers Group: https://www.facebook.com/groups/1287348628022940/ ;

You can always drop me an email. I love to hear from my readers

Email: wendy@wendywangbooks.com

Thank you again for reading!

Made in the USA
Coppell, TX
29 December 2020